RUTH'S CHOICES

A Journey Of The Heart

E. Ruth Harder

A Russian Hill Press Book
United States • United Kingdom • Australia

Russian Hill Press

The publisher is not responsible for websites
(or their content) that are not owned by the publisher.

Copyright © 2025 by E. Ruth Harder
Cover and Book Designer: Coleen Royal

Library of Congress Control Number: 2025904210
ISBN: 979-8-9879285-8-5 (softcover)
ISBN: 979-8-9879285-9-2 (ebook)

Quotations Source: *Holy Bible, New Revised Standard Version,*
Augsburg Fortress, 1990

Dedication

This book is dedicated in thankfulness to my dear children, Chip and Christy, Coleen and J, Debby and Rod, who have supported me in so many ways as I age.

Acknowledgements

Many people helped me in the creation and publication of Ruth's Choices: A Journey of the Heart.

I am thankful to all who encouraged me to write: my children, grandchildren, sisters and friends, and the Holy Cross Lutheran church family in Livermore California.

Dear fellow writer, Patricia Boyle beta read and edited my manuscript with great care and insight. I am very grateful to her as I could not have done it nearly so well without her help.

I am blessed to have Coleen Royal, who created my fabulous cover design as well as the book's interior design. She is not only a talented artist, but also my daughter.

I'm indebted to Paula Chinick of Russian Hill Press who provides a valuable service.

To God be the glory, because without his guidance I could not have created this work of Biblical historical fiction.

History Of Ruth

Why is the book of Ruth in the Old Testament important? Some have used Ruth's promise to Naomi when she went from Moab to Jerusalem as a reading at weddings. It is a good way to think about the book as the scripture promises that wherever the partner goes they will go with them, and live, and that they will worship the same God.

The most important Biblical historical reason is that Ruth and Boaz have a son named Obed, and he is the father of Jesse, who was the father of King David. All the firstborn men in the lineage are direct descendants of Joseph, the earthly father of Jesus, whose wife Mary was a cousin of Joseph.

Matthew 1: 1-17

1 An account of genealogy of Jesus the Messiah, the son of David, the son of Abraham.

2 Abraham was the father of Isaac, the father of Jacob, and Jacob the father of Judah,

3 and Judah the father of Perez and Zerah by Tamar, and Perez the father of Hezron, and Hezron the father of Aram,

4 and Aram the father of Aminadab, and Aminadab the father of Nashon, and Nashon the father of Salmon,

5 and Salmon the father of Boaz by Rahab, and Boaz the father of Obed by Ruth, and Obed the father of Jesse,

6 and Jesse the father of King David. And David was the father of Solomon by Bathsheba Uriah's wife,

7 and Solomon the father of Rehoboam, and Rehoboam the father of Abijah, and Abijah the father of Asaph,

8 and Asaph the father of Jehoshaphat, and Jehoshaphat the father of Uzziah,

9 And Uzziah the father of Ahaz, and Ahaz the father of Hezekiah,

10 and Hezekiah the father of Manasseh, and Manasseh the father of Amos,

11 and Amos the father of Josiah, the father of Jechoniah and his brothers at the time of deportation to Babylon.

12 After the deportation to Babylon, Jechoniah was the father of Salathiel,

13 and Salathiel the father of Abiud, and Abiud the father of Eliakim. And Eliakim the father of Azor.

14 And Azor the father of Achim, and Achim the father of Eliud,

15 and Eliud the father of Eleazar, and Eleazar the father of Matthan, and Matthan the father of Jacob,

16 And Jacob the father of Joseph the husband of Mary, of whom Jesus was born, who is called the Messiah.

17 So all the generations from Abraham to David are fourteen generations; and from David to the deportation to Babylon are fourteen generations; and from the deportation to Babylon to the Messiah are fourteen generations.

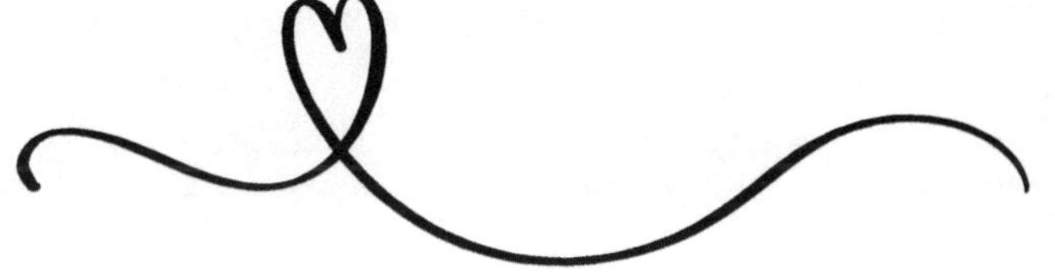

RUTH'S CHOICES

A Journey Of The Heart

1. Naomi

Trust in him at all times, O people;
Pour out your heart before him;
God is a refuge for us.

Psalm 62: 8

The tension unsettled me and surrounded me. The air was still and dry on our lands outside of Bethlehem. Elimelech faced me as we sat on a stone bench in front of our wood and gray stone house, and spoke in an aggrieved voice, "I cannot hold onto our lands and cattle here any longer. My land will still be here, but we cannot stay and maintain it. I kept hoping Yahweh would answer our many prayerful sacrifices and send rain on our stunted and dry crops. There is not even one green leaf in the barley, spelt, or the grazing land for our sheep."

I wanted to weep at the thought. "Where is the faith in Yahweh we have always relied on to provide for us? How can we leave? Where would we go? Bethlehem is our home and all our family and friends are here."

Elimelech turned away from me, cupped his hands and buried his face so I would not see his anguish. "Our sheep bawl with thirst for green grass. Where crops grew there is a wasteland of dust the wind sweeps into the air with devilish swirls. Soon, we too will cry with thirst and hunger. A few have left. We cannot stay here and starve." He composed himself and looked at me earnestly. "I have heard good reports from the land of Moab. It is verdant with ample water for crops and animals. Our neighbor Josiah to the west of our property has gathered his family, his animals, and stored grain. He has loaded it all on donkeys, oxen and carts. His family is traveling there, hoping for a better future for his sons. The dust their cart wheels fling into the air hangs and waits for moisture which is not there."

"I know our people have always found a way to survive, even when they were exiled in a distant land. But can we not last another season and see if the rains will return? The people in Moab worship Chemosh, not Yahweh. What if our sons marry wives there and turn to a foreign deity?"

Elimelech only shook his head from side to side and said nothing else. There was no use to dissuade him once he had a plan in his mind, so I did not tell him of all my misgivings and sadness. I watched as our slaves and hired men rounded up the sheep, the oxen, the milk goats, and donkeys. All were organized with the skill of Elimelech and our two young sons, Mahlon and Chilion. I reluctantly started packing up the household items I thought we would need for the trip and then to set up another home in Moab. My house servant helped but said she would not come with us as she had a family who would not go with her.

It soon came to pass we were all walking or riding on the long dusty, rocky trail to the land of Moab. Some of our distant relatives had settled there so very long ago. For many years there was much strife between Judah and Moab, but time had passed and there were more peaceful relations now.

As we traveled on the dirty and sometimes hot trail, the dust settled on everything in the cart and I soon resigned myself to only shake things clean when we stopped. My thoughts fled to how I would be able to speak with the people since I did not know the Moabite language. Two of our hired herders had ties to Moab and knew the language. They were teaching our sons, sometimes teasing them with wrong word meanings, yet the boys learned much. Elimelech seemed to know many languages from years of dealing with others near and far. I was not so learned, but trusted Yahweh was leading us to this new place and He would provide.

Early one morning, I was startled awake on my blanket bed in our cart by loud noises outside. Men were yelling, animals were braying, and general confusion filled the air. I trembled with fear. Elimelech said, "Be still Naomi. I will take care of this." I remained on my sleeping mat in the cart, as my life pulse drummed in my chest.

We had been beset by men who stole some of our flock of sheep. The hired men tried to beat them off with sticks, but could not prevail against the band of evil men. Alas, some of our sheep and milk goats were herded away as well as one of our best donkeys. Elimelech sat beside me after all had settled down. He said, "Our herdsmen Eggar and Ham were keeping watch, but there were at least eight men who came upon us suddenly before daybreak. Try as they might, the men overpowered them before Mahlon and some of the others were awakened and helped repel the robbers. They did not look for money or goods, but only wanted our sheep and other livestock. Not all of them were taken, only less than half of our numerous flock of sheep. No one was killed or physically harmed. Only one herder stumbled and injured his ankle, so will not walk for a few days. The remaining animals can be easily tended by the rest of the herders." Every night when we stopped, there was a makeshift trough set out with water for the animals, and another with hay.

I touched Elimelech's arm affectionately and said, "I will make us all some porridge for breakfast if there are enough coals from last night to make a fire. We also must thank Yahweh for saving us from more harm from those men. No one was slain. We cannot linger here as the evil men may return." My nose caught a whiff of smoke. A fire had already been kindled by our servants where we camped, so coals were ready for me to cook food.

While we were all disheartened by the theft, it served as a warning to be ever vigilant as we continued. Elimelech decided that three servants as well as either Mahlon or he would keep night watch from now on in our journey. We were thankful we had no further incidents of theft as we continued our trek.

The trail seemed endless. Some days I thought we would never get where we intended to go, and I remembered the story of how our people had wandered from Egypt in the wilderness for about forty years before they came to the land where our people were finally established. I worried when some ewes bore lambs which did not live; a donkey fell and broke her leg so could not continue and had to be destroyed.

I felt vulnerable, but kept up as best I could, cooking nourishing food when we stopped.

Lightening flashed beneath dark clouds in the distance as we walked and thunder crashed as a storm neared. Elimelech was almost overjoyed with the thought of rain as we had not seen any for so very long. But we were already far from our lands and nearing the area where we intended to settle our family. The herders gathered the flocks into one big company so they could be more easily protected. We secured meal and food and anything else needing protection beneath covers or inside the cart. I stayed inside and held an orphan lamb tucked into my cape on my lap. Another ewe would soon give birth and we would give her the orphan to feed as well as her own. Its fresh woolly warmth was cuddly to my touch and its mellow aroma filled my senses as it looked up at me with sleepy dark eyes. I wished it was a grandchild. I secretly longed for a daughter, but would have to settle for daughters-in-law. My sons were not yet old enough to marry, and I smiled wistfully. I wondered now if we would select Moabite girls for their brides, or if there might be daughters in a family from Judah who had come on the same trek to flee the drought. I slept, dreaming of the future.

One morning when I awakened, I saw the terrain rise high up in the near distance which would be our new abode, the mesa known as Moab. My heart sang praise to Yahweh. He was providing for us a place. I prayed we would be accepted there and not driven away.

Elimelech came to me to acknowledge hope lay before us. I could not help it; I sobbed. My tears were half worry about the future, half joy our journey would soon be over. My family and I had survived along with servants who had come with us.

Elimelech and two hired men went ahead of the rest of us to find a suitable piece of land to purchase. Dust settled as we had a rain shower. It was refreshing, and frolicking like boys at the moment, Mahlon and Chilion went out and opened their mouths to rain.

Our boys were now in charge of herding the sheep up the hill toward Moab. They had taken some responsibility for herding all the while, but now they were in charge. They squared their shoulders and looked older to me somehow. It is a revelation for a mother to realize her little boys are almost men. Had it happened when I wasn't looking? I prayed all would be well.

We arrived at the top of the long road safely, and Elimelech met us as we rounded a curve. "I found us some beautiful fields," he said. He kissed both my cheeks and looked into my eyes for acceptance of what he had done.

"It is good," I said, and gave him a tired smile.

Out of nowhere they appeared, loud shouting men approached us. "Go back where you belong, you Judahites! You don't belong here, you dogs!"

"Men, I cannot go back and subject my wife, my sons and all my sheep and cattle to sure starvation. Have some pity for people who need your neighborliness and good will. I have purchased a plot of land and given money for it. Leave us be at peace."

They refused to listen and waved sticks in the air. One man had a metal spear which he menaced and threatened to throw, as they continued their insistence we should leave.

My cheeks were wet with tears, and I was fearful. I covered my head completely with my woolen scarf. But I knew the hatred we faced would not be easily dissuaded. "What will happen to us?" I whispered.

2. Ruth

In the days when the judges ruled, there was a famine in the land, and a certain man in Bethlehem in Judah went to live in the country of Moab, he and his wife and two sons.

Ruth 1: 1

From my vantage point on the mesa where we lived, I could see people coming up the trail to our city, Kir-Heres, Moab. I lived there with my father and mother, my brother Ammon and younger sister, and we had farm lands outside the city. It was a pleasant day and a breeze blew, tugging at loose strands of my dark hair, and threatening to undo my braids. My long tan wool tunic flapped in the breeze as I stood watching. The nearby grain crop was turning from green to gold, its earthy scent in the air, and workmen were chasing away vermin from the crop. I heard their stomping and calls to each other. It was all part of my ordinary life, and I felt safe and secure in the small village. Sometimes I felt a restlessness, and an urgency for something different.

I had never been anywhere besides Moab, the country where I lived. Adventure was what I craved. While my parents made comments, I was not sure why all the people were coming from Judah to live among us. I envied them. They could have a whole new experience from the lives they had lived in their former country. The trek must have been exciting, especially for the people my age who may never have been away from their usual living place before.

My parents said families were coming here to escape a drought and famine in Judah. I watched a woman and two boys trudge up with a donkey, an ox cart, herders, and a herd of sheep and goats. I heard the lowing and baaing of their animals, and distant voices speaking in a tongue of which I understood a few words.

Perhaps the woman was a widow or her husband was already in the area buying land. Following them were men who were tending the animals. I wanted to run and greet them, but shyness overtook me so I did not. Later in the day, my brother Ammon told me the family had come from Bethlehem and would be living nearby. The man, Elimelech, had purchased land on which to live and graze his animals. His place was the one next to Nahum's, which was across from our fields.

"The young men are near your age," Ammon teased.

"It will be two years before I am old enough to be promised to anyone," I retorted, blushing. I picked up a clod of dirt and threw it at him. It did not reach him, and shattered in front of him, and he did not respond in kind, but laughed.

"The thought has crossed your mind." He went to wash before our evening meal.

During our evening repast, my father and Ammon were relating an incident in which the village mean boys had staged an unwelcome party for the newcomers, told them to go back to their home and threatened them with sticks. Ammon had watched at a distance at first, and reported to my father how the man and his two sons had bravely stood their ground. They had not fought back. The man had boldly explained he now was a landowner here and had every right to bring his family onto it to live. His sons and servants continued to herd his sheep forward so the men had to back up, especially when the donkey pulling a cart proceeded as if they were not there. "I admire those people," Ammon said. "It took a lot of courage to travel far and find a good place where they could grow crops and live. Those hecklers are the cowards!"

+++

Days later, I went to the local well to draw water in our stone jar when it was my turn, and my friend Orpah sidled up to me with her water jar teetering on her shoulder. "Did you see the new neighbor family?" Orpah asked with raised eyebrows.

"I watched them come up the trail a few days ago."

"They have two sons, Mahlon and Chilion, who are a little older than us. I have heard tell they are very nice looking."

"Oh, you are interested in a foreigner rather than our local boys from Moab? They probably don't even speak our language."

"Why would it matter as long as they know how to be husbands?"

We giggled at her insinuation and set our water jugs down by the well to draw up the bucket and fill them with water for our mothers.

A pleasant looking woman, wearing a long cream-colored garment, came to draw water, and I wondered if she might be one of the newcomers, but was too shy to ask. Orpah looked at her and said, "Are you our new neighbor?"

"Yes, I am Naomi, wife of Elimelech from Bethlehem in Judah, thank you. My husband, sons and

I have recently come as the place we lived in Bethlehem dried up. Our water wells were dry and crops no longer flourished. We came here where distant kinsmen once lived as we heard the drought and famine had not reached here."

"I am Orpah and this is my friend Ruth. You speak a language we understand a little even though it is not our local Moabite tongue."

"I hope our families can be friends. We are still getting settled here, but one day our families should meet. Perhaps we can help with the harvest," Naomi said, but nothing about the mean boys who had threatened them when they arrived.

When I set the water jug down in our kitchen I was almost too excited to tell my mother. "I met a woman at the well, one who has traveled here to live to escape the famine in Judah. Her name is Naomi, and she seems very nice. She offered to help with our harvest."

"Thank you, Ruth. Now would you please pour water into the basin for your father and brother to wash?" I nodded, and did as I was told. Mother did not respond as I had hoped. Families here were upset by all the people arriving to escape the parched areas, and some worried they would take over our lands.

While my father was a distant descendant of Ammon, my mother was of a different tribe who worshipped Chemosh. Father believed in Yahweh, the one Lord of all creation, yet he tolerated and even joined my mother in reverence for other gods. I learned to worship the same way, and, albeit sometimes confusing, accepted the teachings of both my parents. Father had taught me a few words of his ancestral language. My father's name was Abelmoab, and mother's name was Hagareva.

As time went by, Orpah and I looked for ways to spy on Mahlon and Chilion as they tended their sheep in the nearby grasslands. We found small bushes to hide behind and sat eating dates and figs to pass the time. The gentle breeze and warm sunshine lulled me to close my eyes. One day a wooly ewe with her lamb wandered over where we were sitting. I exclaimed, "Oh, what a darling lamb." Orpah put her finger to her lips to shush me, but it was too late.

One of the boys was there in a flash and demanded, "What are you doing here? Are you planning to steal the lamb?"

Orpah stood up, "What if I were to take it? What would you do?"

"I would strike you with my staff." He stood tall, making a feeble attempt at menacing us. He had grown a stubble of short dark facial hair, not yet a beard or mustache.

I laughed and stood, a little shorter than Orpah. His dark eyes opened wide. "I am Chilion and my brother over there is Mahlon. You must be our neighbors."

"Yes, but only until your families move back to Judah, which will not be any too soon," Orpah tried to sound like her parents.

"We had no choice, but to leave our home in Bethlehem. Our crops failed to grow, and our animals were dying of thirst. We would have died next. I will try not to offend you. Our father purchased land here."

"I understand you needed to leave your home or else die of thirst there. I am sorry and hope rain returns to your land soon," I said.

"If Yahweh wills," Chilion said and turned to go, but Mahlon strode up. He appeared to be a little older, had a dark trimmed beard and mustache, was more robust, and taller than Chilion. I liked what I saw.

"You have found us a couple of women," Mahlon said, with a wide smile lighting up his handsome bearded face. His brown eyes sparkled as he gazed at me.

I turned to go, but Orpah stood her ground, hands on hips. "You have supposed rightly. We are women."

I pulled on her arm, forcing her to come with me, and we retreated giggling.

"Chilion could not take his eyes off of you," I said.

"Mahlon seemed equally taken with you." Orpah skipped, and I joined her as we went home.

"Chilion was the younger one; I think he may be quieter than Mahlon."

"I think not. We will see in time who speaks, and who does not," Orpah said.

Every day we went to the place to spy on the boys, and soon they were expecting us and tried to trick us into thinking they did not see us. But if a lamb strayed in our direction, Mahlon usually followed it and used it as an excuse to talk with us. I could see the boys were fond of us which might not be good, because one day the family would go back to Judah if rains returned to their land. What if his father asked to have Orpah or me as Mahlon's wife? We would be very sad to live far away from each other.

One day Orpah said, "Ruth, let us not go up to the grazing boys today. I am tired of the game we started by going and spying on them. I saw wild flowers blooming we could go pick."

"Very well, but you know they will miss us. It distracts them from the sameness of sheep and more sheep." We giggled.

We went to gather flowers then, the last yellow and white ones. Some were already drying in the sun. Our meager bouquets we brought home and displayed on our front porches.

Orpah had been right. Mahlon and Chilion made no attempt to ignore us when we came the next time. "Where were you?" Mahlon asked.

"Why would you care?" Orpah retorted.

He paused, then answered. "I do care what happens to you women."

Orpah is seldom at a loss for words, but his answer caused her to be silent. She reddened.

I giggled at the interaction, but she did not join me.

"Have any lambs gone astray?" I asked.

"Only the two of you." Mahlon turned quickly and went back to his brother and the sheep.

I smiled. "He has a quick wit."

"I agree," Orpah said.

3. Naomi

If I take the wings of the morning and settle in the farthest limits of the sea, even there your hand shall lead me, and your right hand shall hold me fast.

Psalm 139: 9-10

We had been in Moab for four years and things were going well. Elimelech asked, "Shall we arrange for our boys to have property? Mahlon has become very capable and asked me if he could obtain some land of his own to farm as he was interested in growing barley. There is a nearby farm for sale. Once he has established himself as a farmer, we could look for a wife for him."

"We will help him begin his own livelihood here if it is what he wishes. I do not know when we will be able to return to Bethlehem, or if we ever will." I said. "Both sons will be treated the same, as Chilion favors crop and grassy lands where he can graze sheep."

When those business transactions were completed, and Mahlon and Chilion had their land, Mahlon came to us and inquired, "Would you arrange for a bride for me? I am ready to have a woman with me to bear my children. May I be bold to ask? I have a suggestion for one who lives not far from us. Her name is Ruth."

"A lovely girl, and there is no law against our boys marrying Moabite women. Her mother is reserved and polite when I have met her in the town, and her father worships Yahweh," I said. I had spoken with Ruth and her friend Orpah a few times when we went to the well to get water at the same time.

"I do not know when we will go back to Bethlehem to select suitable young women, so I suppose it is all we can do." Elimelech said. "I trust our sons are strong enough in their faith, they will not be swayed into worshipping Chemosh."

"I pray the same, Elimelech." The very thought had been one of my misgivings about traveling afar to Moab to settle here. I knelt at evening prayer time and asked Yahweh to protect my sons.

Elimelech reached an agreement with Ruth's father to have her become Mahlon's wife. They settled on a generous bride price. It was wonderful to think I might have grandchildren to tug at my skirts and little ones for Elimelech to dandle on his knee. Joyfully, we began to make plans for the wedding with both our families in agreement. Ruth's mother, though not glad her daughter would marry a foreigner, was happy her daughter would not be going afar to wed, but be in the near neighborhood. We received reports how our Bethlehem lands were still very dry, so we would not be leaving here very soon.

I missed family and friends I had left there, and often lamented I had needed to leave the place where I had grown up, married, and had children. Here, we had made a few friends, but many did not speak Aramaic, and almost all of them worshipped Chemosh. Elimelech told me Ruth's father worshipped Yahweh, but had few people with whom to worship, and her mother was devoted to Chemosh. I truly worried what would happen to my children and our grandchildren were they not trained to have faith in Yahweh as my sons had been.

4. Ruth

Many waters cannot quench love, neither can floods drown it. If one offered for love all the wealth of his house, it would be utterly scorned.

Song of Solomon 8:7

As some years elapsed, one day I hurried to see Orpah at the corners of our properties where we usually met. I had a huge smile on my face. "It has happened. Elimelech met with my father and asked if I could become Mahlon's wife. They told me, because my mother insisted since they are foreigners I should be consulted before the agreement was final. The transaction is taking place. I am excited and scared at the same time. I do want to marry Mahlon and have a family. He is so handsome! I only hope we will live here and not go to Judah even if the drought and famine ends there."

"No matter where you live, we will still be friends," Orpah said. "Or you could hide me among your things when you go," she continued with a lilt of mischief in her voice. Orpah hugged me. I wondered at how dear had been the bride price for me, because when the families from the drought area had started moving here, my parents, especially mother, had been so adamantly against them. Time must have softened things.

A few days after my announcement, Orpah's parents made agreement with Elimelech for her to be wedded to Chilion. We squealed and hugged again at the news. The wedding celebrations would take place together as Orpah and I both wanted it, our parents agreed, and the brothers' parents were happy to do the same. My parents and Orpah's family got along well, so it was easy to have the weddings happen together. And having one feast and wedding celebration would be less costly to everyone.

Orpah and I were excited and talked of nothing else when we were together, mostly discussing what we would wear. We wanted matching robes, with the same colors, but our mothers begged us to be dressed similarly if we wished, but not identical. "Maybe they are afraid we would confuse our husbands," Orpah said. We both rolled on the mat we sat upon overcome with gales of laughter. Our parents made all the food plans and we had no say in it. Soon the day came when all the activity began.

The wedding celebration lasted a week including the day before the ceremony when all was being made ready and people had begun to arrive at the home of Naomi and Elimelech where the wedding would take place, and where we would all live. Naomi had set out colorful pots with green plants and some flowers.

The wind gusted across the harvested fields, blowing dust and chaff high in the air like flocks of birds going away for the next season. It seemed like an omen of sorts. It was not birds. Not many species seemed to linger as we had few trees. They nested in the shallow hollows of the earth among stubble. I felt excited and fearful at the same time. I couldn't name what I was afraid of had anyone asked. As I put on my happiest smile, it hid all my innermost thoughts. It was my friend's special day as well as mine, and I would not risk any words to spoil her joy. The day came for the celebrations to begin.

"Ruth, this is it," she exclaimed. "You look more

beautiful all dressed up."

"Your dyed yellow and red linen robe suit you very well," I said. I thought how costly her flaxen garment, traded from afar, must have been. More local and practical, I wore an outer woven tan wool robe with a red sash, with the tunic beneath a soft cream wool. My hair was combed and braided to form a crown and the rest of my long hair flowed in a cascade of dark waves down my back. Orpah's was styled the same. Neither of us had ever cut our hair so it was very long. Bright ribbons and fresh flowers decorated our "crowns."

"Look at us! We are twin queens with fresh crowns." Orpah said. As was a custom in Moab, my head, as well as Orpah's was covered with a fine cloth to hide our faces on our wedding day until the ceremony. It was similar to the custom they had in Bethlehem where Naomi and her family were from.

We were allowed to wait together in a tent after all the fussing and decorating of ourselves by our mothers and servants had taken place. We giggled nervously and Orpah made silly remarks about Mahlon and Chilion. "Will Chilion be up herding sheep tomorrow morning?"

"I do not think so!" I said. "He will probably be too sore to move after spending the night with you."

"After all the dancing, we will be too exhausted to do anything but sleep. Chilion, the quiet one, will be the one to save some energy for his bride," I said.

Orpah reddened. "Will he know what to do?"

"You can teach him if you know what you are both to be doing!"

We laughed, throwing our heads back unthinking. Orpah lost some of the red flowers from her crown, and I accidentally undid a ribbon. We quieted. "I'll repair your crown, if I may." I picked up the red flowers, and began to put them back. "But you have to re-tie my white ribbon."

Our repairs done, I closed my eyes, sitting on a tan wool cushion. Orpah sighed impatiently. We listened to the music and all the activity outside as people danced, drank wine, laughed and visited.

"Why do we have to miss out on the early part of the fun?" Orpah said. She rolled her head back again, but the flowers stayed in place.

"What if we were to sneak out and join in the fun. Would our mothers rush us back into our hiding place?" I said. We both laughed at the thought.

Orpah could not stop laughing, and said, "If we came out now, would they forbid us to marry?"

Laughing, I said, "Mahlon and Chilion would be very upset if they did."

"After all, they are missing an entire week herding sheep," Orpah said, giggling. And soon it was time for our ceremony.

+++

The canopy had been set and Mahlon and I were the first to recite our duties to each other according to the Ketubah.

Mahlon promised: to feed his wife; clothe her; and provide her conjugal needs. His estate is obligated to pay her a lump sum in the event that he divorces her or dies before she does. He must pay her medical bills if she falls ill; and ransom her if she is taken hostage. If the wife passes away before the husband, he must pay her burial expenses, and after he dies, her children inherit their mother's ketubah money before the rest of the estate is divided amongst all the heirs. In the event that the husband dies before the wife, she is entitled to live in his home and live off his estate until she dies or remarries, and her daughters, too, are supported by his estate until they marry.

It all sounded like a bunch of words to me, and I heard the part about me being able to stay in his home if he died, and thought it was completely unlikely to happen any time soon.

My part was simply to respect my husband, which I had been told by my mother meant I was to obey him, go to bed with him when he asked, and direct the household servants. Chilion and Orpah recited the same words to each other.

Flutes played, drums beat, and we all formed circles to dance. The women were swept into a hora circle. The boys and men boisterously kicked up their heels and carried Mahlon and Chilion up over their heads, handing them off from one to another and threatening to drop them. A lot of laughter and whoops of joy echoed long into the night. I had been so elated, and now my wedding had actually happened I was feeling a tiredness I had not expected. Perhaps I needed a handful of dates to give me energy. I smiled and walked toward the food table.

In a blur, I thought the activity had stopped or slowed, and I was not sure why until I saw Mahlon and Chilion rush to their father's side.

5. Naomi

Be gracious to me, O Lord, for I am in distress; my eye wastes away with grief, and my soul and body also.
For my life is spent with sorrow, and my years with sighing; my strength fails because of my misery, and my bones waste away.

Psalm 31: 9-10

As was our custom, our children would live in two dwellings which would be attached to our house. Construction of the homes for our sons and their families began immediately after wedding plans were made. We hired the village men who had helped Elimelech and our sons build our home when we had arrived. They laid baked brick and stones to erect dwellings attached to our house. Much activity occurred and I often made tea and date cakes, or wine and bread for them to eat while they worked. It was finally done. A trader in rugs and household items came with samples for me to select for the new couples. I chose what I hoped they would like.

+++

A canopy was erected for the ceremonies for the weddings. Lambs were slaughtered for roasting, vegetables and fruits were piled high on tables in order to feed the many wedding guests. Our boys were marrying girls who were already best friends, so there would be little strife as we all would live together in different parts of the same abode. I was only saddened by our relatives back in Bethlehem not being here. We were elated by the festivities which had been planned by our three families. As all the details were handled, I noticed Elimelech was more tired and worn out than he had ever been.

During the celebration of the marriages, we all danced lively dances to tambourines, drums, whistles, and lyres. I joined in the hora circle of women with the brides. Elimelech was with the boisterous men as much as he could, but often sat out of the frolic. When we were dancing as the day wore on, Elimelech and I were smiling and dancing around each other clapping our hands. He was breathing with difficulty as he knelt submissively before me, to dance on his knees as was a custom for the particular dance. But he no longer danced, he clutched at his chest. Others may not have noticed what was happening, but Orpah's father, who was a seer, rushed to his side and helped him to the shade. I fanned his face, and another guest brought a cool cloth to place on his forehead. Another man brought wine for him to sip. Both our sons rushed to him with frowns of worry to inquire how he fared. Elimelech stood, and reassured them he was only a little tired from all the dancing, clapped them on the shoulders. "Enjoy your day and do not be concerned about me."

The wedding celebrations continued as everyone thought he was simply tired from all the activities. Our sons and their brides had married. We felt joyful, but Elimelech often sat and did not visit as we should have been with guests. The celebration was a beautiful highlight. And I was delighted neighbors had all come to celebrate with us. Even our neighbor Nahum and his wife had come, but not their little ones. Soon it was over and all the guests left us. Our children went to their rooms of the house which had been built and prepared for them to live. I felt happy and relieved it had all gone so well.

The next morning, I awakened early to see Elimelech still abed, appearing to be peaceful and very quiet. I began to make our morning porridge, but a sudden chill seized me. I went to rouse my husband, and saw he was breathing, but not deeply. I knelt at his side weeping, and squeezed his hand. His eyes fluttered open and closed, and he sighed, "Naomi." In an instant, he breathed no more. I collapsed in tears as I could not believe what had happened in those few moments. I wondered how I would carry on without him, save for my two sons and their new wives.

Our dancing had turned to mourning and our children felt the full impact of their father's absence. We spent seven days sitting shiva in a foreign land. Neighbors who did not all believe in Yahweh as we did, came out of respect for Elimelech, and to sympathize with our family.

"I think we will never go back to Bethlehem," Chilion said. "Now we have our father's cattle and lands to manage as well as our own."

"Ever the pessimist, brother," Mahlon said. "When we have sons, we will bring our families back to Bethlehem." He smiled, and clapped his brother on the shoulder.

My sons worked hard as did their wives to make a living from their harvests and sheep. Orpah often went to her parent's home for a short visit. Ruth did not go see her parents as often. She got along well with me and we cooked together for all of us as we ate at a common table.

As time elapsed, I watched my daughters-in-law hoping one day to see them both with bodies rounded in happy expectation of sons. I could hardly wait for the day a grandchild would be born.

6. Ruth

For surely, I know the plans I have for you, says the Lord,
plans for your welfare and not for harm, to give
you a future with hope.

Jeremiah 29: 11

Mahlon was a wonderful husband and good companion to me. He respected my wishes. If I wanted our room arranged in a certain way, he said, "I will be satisfied if I know you are happy with the bed on the far wall, and the chairs located where you wish." Even though Naomi had chosen one large rug in a leaf swirl design for us to use, I could choose the many-colored rugs I liked and the warm natural colored blankets.

Naomi treated me like a daughter, and showed me her way of making lamb stew, which herbs to use, and the like. I helped as much as I could in the kitchen as my rooms with Mahlon needed little care. Naomi walked with Orpah and me to find herbs for cooking, showed us a place near narrow mountain stream where certain mushrooms grew which were good to eat. I liked Naomi and she told both of us girls she loved us.

Orpah and I constantly checked with each other whether there were any signs either of us was "with child." One morning she had not come to have morning porridge with the rest of us. Chilion said she felt ill as he left to herd sheep. After we had finished cleaning the dishes, I went to Orpah's rooms opposite ours and knocked on her door. "Get up lazy one." I said gently. I heard her shuffling to the door and she opened it a crack, then let me in.

I had brought her some mint tea Naomi had made. She wrapped her hands around the plain ceramic bowl, enjoyed the warmth on her hands. "I do not know what is happening in my insides to make me upset," she said.

Naomi had given me the tea to take to Orpah, smiled, and said, "Perhaps she has an illness, but it may be something else." I had heard women speak of it before. Sometimes when one's womb is opened and life is being started there, one's body responds with upset ailments. I understood the hope in Naomi's smile.

I could not wait to ask Orpah. "Are you with child?"

"I do not know," she moaned. She took a sip of the tea. "My moon cycle did not happen as expected for a few weeks. I could be ill because of it."

"Does it mean you may be with child?" I did not know how everything worked. "We should ask Naomi. She bore two sons."

"You ask her. I do not feel like talking with anyone. Besides, you are her favorite daughter-in-law."

"She loves us both the same, and I have not seen her favoring me. If you were to bring her a grandson, she would surely favor you!"

Orpah brightened up with our conversation. I saw more color in her cheeks as she sipped the tea. She lay back down, and I tucked her in, kissed her cheek and returned to Naomi.

When I went to the common well for water, Orpah's mother was there and asked if Orpah was being made a slave in Naomi's house.

"We are both treated well, but today Orpah has a stomach ailment," I said.

"Oh," she exclaimed, "so soon."

I cocked my head in question, but did not ask.

"She may be going to have a baby. My daughter will be a mother! I am almost sure of it as Orpah is never ill."

I did not want to appear ignorant of common knowledge, so I kept my questions to myself and bid her a good day, took up my full water jar and left. I would have skipped and frolicked thinking about a baby had I not been carrying water.

I set the water in the kitchen by Naomi and ran to Orpah's room, burst in without knocking, and exclaimed, "You are going to have a baby!"

"Oh, and how do you know this?" She sat up, squared her shoulders with a surprised, albeit sour look on her face.

"Your mother was getting water at the same time I was and asked how you were and I told her you were ill, and she got excited and practically declared you were with child."

Orpah laughed, throwing her head back as we had at some funny thing when we were growing up together. I laughed too. We hugged. "It is probably too soon to tell Chilion," she said. "What if we are wrong and this is some other ailment?"

"Your mother thinks it is possibly a baby," I said. "Will she put the news out to others?"

"I am not sure what she will do, but I expect I will have a visit from her very soon."

As time passed, and Orpah finally got over her stomach ills, her breasts and middle body grew in size.

Naomi made sure she had special food which would keep the baby growing inside of her healthy. Goat milk and cheese, bread dripping with honey, lentils and lamb stew laden with vegetables were placed in abundance before her and the rest of us at the table. The family also watched me without comment, but I knew they were waiting for Mahlon and me to follow in like manner to be "with child."

When Orpah felt the small stirrings in her belly, she would come to me and tell me the butterfly was moving about in her womb. I asked her if it might not be bloat from all the foods she was eating. We laughed at the thought. Her face had become more rounded, and skin blossomed with color. We two were enjoying the experience together, even though I wished it was happening it in my body too. Would Yahweh ever open my womb? According to Naomi it was what needed to happen.

As the days were accomplished so it was time for the baby to come, Naomi brought an older woman, Amah, who often attended births. Orpah squatted on a birth stool which had a wool lined basin to catch the blood and the child. I was not in the room while the birth took place, but I heard Orpah crying out in pain as the child was being born. Afterwards, Amah cleaned the birthing area and took the remains in the basin to be buried properly.

I watched Naomi wash the baby with salted water and swaddle it in a warm wool cloth. I looked at her without asking the question, but she answered me, "Orpah has borne a beautiful girl child. Her name will be Hester."

"Will Chilion be disappointed it was not a son?"

"I do not think so, as he has many more years to produce sons."

I smiled, remembering a discussion I had with Orpah while she was great with child. I had asked if she preferred a boy or girl for her firstborn, and she had said it did not matter because she had more childbearing years to come. She giggled then and had told me Mahlon and I ought to get busy and produce an heir and a play friend for her baby. I had shaken my head, and told her it was not for not trying we had no sign of a child coming. I will admit I was disappointed at so far being barren. It was not what I had imagined for my life.

7. Naomi

Those who love me, I will deliver;
I will protect those who know my name,
When they call to me, I will answer them,
I will be with them in trouble,
I will rescue them and honor them.

Psalm 91: 14–15

Ruth's womb as yet remained closed. We all cuddled and held Hester and played with her. She had begun to smile and gurgle sweet noises as I sang to her. I was truly blessed. I wished Elimelech were here to see the little one and dandle her on his knee. I smiled remembering how he had often talked about his sons having children so his lineage would continue on. I rocked Hester in my arms as I walked to and fro with her, and thought nothing could spoil my joy. The happy feeling did not last.

A breathing sickness plagued the area. Chilion succumbed to it first and soon our little Hester suffered and breathed her last breath. With much weeping, we buried them in our hewn cave-like family tomb where Elimelech was buried. Orpah remained with me and the rest of the family. Although deeply mourning, she tried to understand our way of sitting shiva seven days since she had grown up in a household which worshipped Chemosh, not Yahweh. A mother is not supposed to see her children die. It is as if the whole world is backwards. I could not get my grief under control. I had been unduly punished by Yahweh, and did not know why. While I cried silently to myself in my room I resolved to remain strong for Orpah and the rest of the family, but could not smile. Little did I know what else awaited me.

Mahlon remained strong despite his grief and was stoic during the days of sitting shiva. He had the burden of not only his father's land, his mother, his sister-in-law and Chilion's property, but his own land. Mahlon often went down the mountain to obtain supplies. One time he seemed to be delayed for a very long while, and we wondered what had happened to keep him detained. Had Chilion been alive, I would have sent him to look for his brother.

We did not know anything until a traveler from our village found his and his servant's animal-ravaged bodies, and what was left of his empty cart in a ravine beside the road. He had been the victim of robbers. Whether they caused him to career off the road into the ravine or robbed what was left afterwards no one could tell. I would not believe what I was hearing the man say until he made me sit on my bench, and then he repeated it with deep sympathy. I breathed in and out rapidly to control my voice, but I finally screamed out something neither I nor anyone listening could understand. I had too much sadness to bear.

Ruth collapsed on her mat, and Orpah put her arms around her friend to console her as they wept together. Now they were both young widows. In the next days as we sat shiva, Ruth was beside herself with grief, but stayed with Orpah and me. Mahlon's bones were placed in an ossuary since the flesh was gone and dried up. His bones were placed in the family tomb with the others.

We women remained together grieving as widows, and trying to hold on with the help of the field servants. We were so deeply struck with grief we could not move normally. While we remained as strong as we could, we did not know what we would do. One day, a man on a donkey rode up the trail to Moab with the news the dryness and famine in Bethlehem had abated. I had a few relatives and Elimelech's land to which I could return. I felt bitter, having lost everything I had, with no husband or sons, only my two lovely daughters-in-law.

I decided to return to Bethlehem. In Kir-Heres of Moab, I sold the land and animals, except for a goat, a pair of oxen and a cart. Neighbor Nahum bought our fields adjoining his as he said he knew how well Elimelech had cared for his property. He would also acquire our house as it was larger than his and he had a big family. One house servant, Petros, and his wife Oma remained with us as we readied ourselves to move.

Our two servants, with Ruth and Orpah, helped me pack what was needed, and we set out on the long trek toward Bethlehem, with oxen pulling a cart loaded with our household goods. As we started traveling, I thought about the welfare of my daughters-in-law. I would now be subjecting them to come with me to a land foreign to them. I begged them, "Please leave me go, turn back and go to your own parents. Perhaps you will find new husbands." They both wept aloud, and it was difficult for me to see them grieved. They clung to each other.

I admonished them again to go to their mothers, then the girls shed more tears. After going a short way, Orpah hugged me tightly as well as Ruth. "Are you coming with me?" She asked Ruth, who did not answer. "You always told me you wanted to go afar for an adventure, now you have your wish. I will miss you." Both of them had tears in their eyes and hugged each other again.

"To have an adventure is not the main reason I will go with Naomi," Ruth said, and turned away from Orpah, who walked back toward Moab to her parents. Ruth looked at me sorrowfully, held me and said, "I am your daughter now, and cannot let you go alone. Entreat me not to leave you or forsake you. Wherever you go I will go, wherever you lodge I will lodge. Your people will be my people, and your God, Yahweh, will be my God."

After our men had all died, Ruth had asked why Yahweh would have allowed it to happen. I had no answer for her, as I often wondered the same. While it did my heart good to know Ruth loved me and cared to stay with me as if she were my daughter, I felt bad for her leaving her own family and her dear friend Orpah. Perhaps Yahweh had a plan, but I could not imagine what it would be. Ruth had begun to believe in Yahweh and worship with us, so it would have been difficult for her to go back to the idols and Chemosh her mother worshipped. I knew not what was ahead for me on the trek, or when I returned to Bethlehem.

"Call me Mara, for I am bitter." I said.

8. Ruth

*When Naomi saw that Ruth was determined to
go with her, she said no more to her.
So the two of them went on until they came to Bethlehem.
When they came to Bethlehem, the whole town was stirred
because of them; and the women said, "Is this Naomi?"*

Ruth 1: 18-19

I was excited, as I started out on the trip to Bethlehem with Naomi. Trees I had never seen before appeared as the trail on which we traveled sloped away from where I had always lived. Small animals scurried away into the grass and bushes as our cart approached. A flock of birds flew over us in a haze of gray. Such was our trek so far, but we had only begun a short while. I hoped for more adventure ahead. Joy filled me even though I was a little sad leaving everything I had ever known, including Orpah. It was a safe and scenic trek. Naomi had been sad at first, but as days passed and our skies were mostly sunny, she seemed to be more at ease. She said, "Yahweh has sent an angel to watch over our travels. While I do not know what I had done to cause all the grief we have had, perhaps now I have found favor with him."

When Mahlon and I were betrothed and married, we were very young. Now I was a young woman with responsibilities for my mother-in-law going to a place which was new to me, but where she knew people and had a history. Bethlehem came into view, and it was surrounded by fields of grain and grazing. When we arrived, I saw the bright sea of barley ripening or already full and ready for harvest. It looked like a sea of gold. Men were in the field with scythes to cut the bundles of sheaves. They would bring them in to the barn for threshing out the grain to be stored to use throughout the months ahead. Breads and porridges would be made of flour ground from the grain for family meals.

Women were in the field gleaning, some walking a row or more behind the men who were cutting off barley sheaves. The women picked up what was left on the ground and bound it into bundles. Some used a length of old cloth, others a basket to hold the grain heads. I watched with great interest in what they were doing and decided it might be a way for me to be more useful to Naomi.

Instead of going to the house she had lived in before she and Elimelech left, we settled in a house in Bethlehem which was small, but enough for two women to reside in comfortably. Naomi had been welcomed by people who knew her and her family before the drought. Women remarked how the years had changed Naomi. A neighbor said, "Deep sadness has put wrinkles on her brow." She had grown grayer hair. Our small abode had once been the home of a couple who had left during the famine and never returned. The mother of the young woman lived next door and was still grieved, but never lost hope her daughter and husband would return. "As of now I want someone to live there and take care of it." She looked directly at me when she said it.

I tried to keep busy, but there was little to do. One morning I said, "Mother Naomi, I see women in the fields picking up barley heads the reapers have dropped. Shall I go and get some for our use?"

"Yes, you may, and try to stay near other women. Not all the men who work the fields are good men." She seldom smiled, but now did, and sounded surprised.

I found a large basket so I could gather the barley heads dropped by the men who were harvesting. As I walked behind the men, other women greeted me warmly, but did not carry on a conversation with me when they heard my Moabite accent. A couple of them avoided looking my way at all.

I saw a tall man, dressed in plain, serviceable raiment, wearing sturdy shoes. He spoke authoritatively to the men and received their respect. I knew he must be an overseer or even the owner of the field. I had gleaned his field all day and was going home to Naomi to let her know when he approached me. I felt shy, wondering if he would ask me to leave and not return since I was a foreigner.

"Daughter, I see you have gleaned some good barley heads today. I want you to stay close to the working women as you gather grain, and do not go to any field but mine." Someone called to him and he left me there. He was a nice-looking older man, tall and well-muscled from work.

I told Naomi about my day. "A man approached me, and told me to come again and glean in his field and no other. He said to stay near the other women in his field. I heard him tell the men to leave me alone, and drop some of the good barley heads for me. He said I could drink of the water jugs provided for the men. His name is Boaz."

Naomi looked at me with great interest and said, "You have found favor. You are gleaning in the field of

Boaz, who is a relative of Elimelech."

The next day, I worked again in his fields. One of the women said to me, "Do not go near the men. Some of them may be rude and not treat women well."

I gleaned for several days. One day, Boaz was in the field working beside the men, bringing in the harvest. He came to me and said, "I have told the men to save a few sheaves for you to have for yourself."

"You are being so kind to me," I said. It was all I could think of to say to this handsome relative of Elimelech.

"You are the one who is kind. I have heard how you left your people in Moab after the death of Naomi's husband and sons, and remained with her as would a daughter. Come sit with me and eat bread and some parched barley. We will dip barley and bread into wine for our meal."

I sat with Boaz, admiring the nice man, whom I now knew was a kinsman. My feet were recovered after sitting there and I continued to work. At day's end, I was tired, but satisfied as I beat out the ephah of barley which I brought home to Naomi.

"Ruth, you are glowing from a day in the field. Wash your hands and we will have our evening repast. Did you see Boaz again today?"

"I did. We sat together at midday and ate parched barley with wine."

She smiled again, then paused and looked up as if she were seeing something on the ceiling, then said,

"My daughter, I have heard tell that Boaz sometimes sleeps on the threshing floor of his barn at day's end. Tomorrow night I want you to go to his barn and do what I tell you to do. Wait until he has eaten and drank his wine and fallen asleep, then go to him and lift the cover from his feet. Sleep at his feet beneath the cover until he awakens. He is not married, and he is Elimelech's relative. If he were to take you as his wife, he would become our family's redeemer."

I sat quietly, not speaking as I took in all she was asking me to do. Is it too bold of me? "What will he think of me when he awakens and finds me there? What is a family redeemer?"

"As the nearest kin left in Elimelech's family, it would be his duty to marry you, receive and farm our property, and preserve Elimelech's family for future generations. When he finds you at his feet, he will know you are agreeing to marry him."

I hesitated, then said, "Yes, Mother, if it is your desire I do this, I will." I trusted Naomi, but I wondered about the wisdom of what she asked me to do. I was attracted to Boaz, and it did not displease me. I wondered what he would do and if he would despise me. He had called me "daughter." Would he scold me? Would he send me away ashamed? I respected my mother-in-law and did not wish to displease her by refusing her request. "What shall I say to him?"

"Tell him to spread his cloak over you for he is next of kin."

The next day after work, I washed myself thoroughly, cleansing all the dust and sweat from my body. I had no perfumes or other fine smelling ointments, but I found a field flower with a pleasant aroma. I tucked it behind my ear, and wore a clean plain tunic and cloak. As darkness descended, I felt anxious when I walked toward the threshing barn of Boaz. Perhaps he would not be there. The chilled breeze bade me wrap my cloak more snugly around myself. Although I had eaten, my stomach felt hollow. As I peered up at the sky, the moon was a crescent, and stars dotted the dark heavens. I took a deep breath and then let it out. Whatever would happen it could be no worse than what had already befallen Naomi and me in the loss of our husbands and her granddaughter Hester. I said a silent prayer to Yahweh in hopes the Lord of heaven and the earth might hear my plea to steady my thoughts and help me do for Naomi what was needed.

The barn was open, so I walked in without incident. I peered inside the dark interior toward the threshing area, hoping to see Boaz. I heard him speak to what appeared to be the last person in the barn besides him, but knew they could not see me. I hid away behind a stack of baskets of unbeaten sheaves and waited. It was quiet except for whispery flutter of wings of some evening birds settling somewhere for the night. I peered out from my hiding place and heard him pouring wine into a cup. I almost imagined I heard him swallowing and chewing. No doubt it was barley bread dipped into wine. I remembered what he had looked like as he savored wine and bread one day with me. I waited longer, and it seemed like a very long time. My insides growled at me as if I had not eaten. My life pulse beat in my chest like drummers at a celebration. I ventured out onto the threshing floor, and thought my knees would give way as I walked barefoot silently, my sandals in my hand. I wondered what would happen.

9. Boaz

Those who go out weeping bearing the seed for sowing, shall come home with shouts of joy, carrying their sheaves.

Psalm 126: 6

Those dry years, it had been a waste to sow seeds on my land. Nothing was growing, not even a weed among wretched dry stubble for two years. The only clouds in the air were dust flung there by the wind. I was as shriveled up in my bones as the surrounding fields. I wanted to marry, but could not expect to do so without an income to provide for a wife and children. The young woman I had in mind was comely, but not too beautiful and vain, and her family were worshippers of Yahweh and lived their faith. I saw her father walking dejectedly as many did those days, and when I spoke to him in Bethlehem he said they would be traveling afar to find a better place to farm and make a living. I gave up hope of asking for his daughter's hand in marriage. I was empty and hurt inside, but knew I must simply bide my time and tend the fields as best I could until Yahweh opened his clouds to pour rain. I had only a handful of necessary yoke of oxen to farm the land and kept a milk goat. I had stored grain and hay to feed them and only hoped it would be enough to last until the drought ended. Water was another matter. I found it necessary to walk a distance to find a well which had not dried. While I thought of going away as so many did, I decided I would stay with the land. A distressing time such as this would be a perfect opening for some foreign power to try to overtake our lands. I would defend my property as well as neighbors who were gone as best I could should it occur.

The hot sun shrank the sparse newly sprouted

barley to sad sprigs on the soil. I surveyed my vast fields which I knew would once again not produce a crop. Cart wheels created dust swirls as families continued to leave in hopes of finding greener country. I watched my kinsman Elimelech and the procession of his family and carts and animals leave our Bethlehem area where all our relatives families had lived for as long as I could remember. A sadness crept into me, threatening to undo my resolve to stay on the land.

Elimelech stopped to speak with me before they left. His jaw was set, but his frowning brow belied his brave move. "We are traveling to Moab where crops are growing due to normal rainfall. I cannot stay here and subject Naomi and my sons to years of near starvation. Even now, we have scraped together every storage of hay and meal for the animals we are bringing with us, and I pray to Yahweh it holds out until we can grow more in the land of Moab. May Yahweh find favor on this land and send rain soon."

"Blessings, I hope it goes well for those big sons you have in a new land where they will not know the language or customs," I said,

"I have heard they worship Chemosh, but otherwise it cannot be much different than our own. Our ancestors, some of whom were Canaanites, lived there before our countries quarreled. It is more peaceful now, and I will buy land and make a new home where we can grow our crops." Elimilech and I grasped our arms farewell. Several years passed since the day I saw them leave. Some years I thought I would not be able to live with disappointment of drought as well as the loneliness since so many neighbors were gone.

All those terribly dry years I never gave up hope. I awakened one morning to a dark cloudy sky, not dust clouds, not light fluffed clouds, but gray and heavy. Yahweh finally reached out his hand and opened his storehouse of water to pour rain upon our parched land. It began with light sprinkling drops and I went out to bask in its coolness. I knelt on the earth and thanked Yahweh for those few drops and pleaded he would send more. Lightning sparked in the sky, thunder rolled like a triumphant bull roaring from the heavens and lightening flashed again. God had answered. As the days progressed, more rain came. I was so overjoyed I sang over and over, "Thank you Yahweh for the rain for our land, for our crops, so we can grow green grass, barley and spelt again. Praise you, Yahweh!" I sometimes whirled around like a madman in the rain, letting myself be drenched. I was so over joyed and prayed it would last. It did, and we could grow grain crops again, those few of us who had stayed and managed to hold on despite the dry years. Grass grew and those who had managed to keep some of their sheep once more could graze.

In recent days, according to the local talk, Elimelech's widow Naomi and one daughter-in-law had returned after Elimelech, his son Chilion and son Mahlon had all died. His land here had remained fallow ten or more years, and his fields grew only weeds and wild grasses, and I meant to inquire about buying the place whenever Naomi was ready.

My barley was ripening in the sun, and I plucked a head, bit into a few grains to test it. I nodded with satisfaction. It was ready to harvest. I called my few slaves to work, and as they began to cut and reap, other reapers saw and joined in. Women from the town came with baskets and bags, hoping to glean what the reapers dropped to take home to their families or sell in the market. My maid servants were out also the second day, gleaning. I rubbed my hands together around a head of barley to open some grains, and inhaled the satisfaction of a blessed harvest. All was well this year. Praise be to Yahweh.

The next day, I saw a young woman with light brown complexion and a long dark braid gleaning in my field. She followed the men, picking up what was dropped. She walked gracefully among the plants, avoided stepping on stubble or stumbling. I had never seen her before, and thought she might be the Moabite daughter-in-law who had been Mahlon's wife, now a widow. She was so young and comely, I wanted to speak with her and warn her to stay with my own servant women who gleaned. I worried because of her beauty and youth the men might take advantage of her.

Field-working men were talking among themselves and chuckling about something, no doubt in a good mood to take pay and food home to their families.

I asked my servant who was in charge of all the reapers who the pretty woman was, and he said she was Naomi's daughter-in-law. Ruth had come back to our area from Moab with Naomi to take care of her. I was touched by hearing of her kindness. Others in town said the same, how out of devotion to Naomi, Ruth had left her own people to come with her mother-in-law.

The next day I approached her and told her I had admonished the men to leave her alone, and whenever she was thirsty she could dip water from the common buckets. I advised her to stay with the women as much as possible. When I talked with my men, I told them to drop extra grain heads for her to pick up, and to allow her to drink from the water buckets I had provided for them.

The next day when I approached Ruth she had a frightened look in her eyes, and bowed low as to an elder. I said, "Don't be afraid of me. Please stay in my fields and do not glean in any other. You will be protected here as I have warned the men not to bother you." I spoke in Aramaic as I didn't speak Moabite, a different Canaanite language, and I hoped she could understand my words.

"Thank you for your kindness," she bowed and spoke in Aramaic which should not have surprised me since she had been living with Naomi.

"Rise, daughter, you have been on your feet all day, working and not stopping. Come sit with me." I motioned to a heap of sheaves. When she sat near me

I was very much aware of her youth, her beauty, her womanliness, but I stopped short of desiring her as she was a young widow of my kinsman's family. We ate barley bread dipped in wine and I drew out some of my parched barley from a pouch at my waist. I shared it all with her companionably. She said little, except to thank me.

I worked along with everyone every day I could. Some days I needed to go into Bethlehem to do business, but otherwise I was in my fields. I saw she came every day and was delighted to see her small frame gliding among the sheaves. I greeted her most days and she greeted me and waved her hand, but she kept working.

Despite my resolve not to be, I was enamored of her. If she had missed even one day, except Sabbath, I would have worried and called on Naomi to find out why. I was too old for one so young. I had missed my chance to marry due to the drought, so had postponed the desire to have a wife and family for years after most men were married. Some families had left the area and others simply stayed to themselves. There were no weddings I can recall during those famine years.

Once it began to rain, I was too busy to think of such things. I plowed, fertilized and planted. I tilled and weeded, all the things I needed to do. As I could I gained slaves and servants to help me in the fields and in my household. I managed my money, my fields, my business. And I worshipped Yahweh in the Synagogue. I knelt for morning prayer at the first watch, when the sun crept to the rim of the earth, and again at the fourth watch, in the evening as the day's light set. On rainy days, I praised Yahweh even more.

We were in the thick of harvest, and I spent a lot of time in the threshing barn at day's end. Some nights I was too exhausted to walk home. I kept a count of all the sheaves and the resulting grain piled up or put into large baskets or bags to be stored or sold. One such night I spread my cloak on the floor atop a soft pile of chaff and lay there in a far corner to sleep. After I ate a small meal and drank wine, I covered myself with a cloak against the coolness of the night, and I fell into the deep sleep of a man who is beyond tired.

10. Ruth

He makes me lie down in green pastures;
He leads me beside still waters;
He restores my soul.
He leads me in right paths for his names sake.

Psalm 23: 2-3

In a far corner of the threshing floor I saw a mound of grain. As I came closer, I heard even breathing, and a light snoring sound. The man's head on a roll of cloth could only be Boaz, the one I hoped to see. He was covered with his large cloak. As I quietly lifted the hem of the cloak, I lay down and hoped I would not awaken him as I slept by his feet. I did not think I would sleep, but I was very tired from working all day.

During the night, Boaz was startled awake when he had turned over, threw aside his cloak, and found me at his feet. I woke up, too. "Who are you?" He demanded. Darkness kept our vision of each other dim.

"I am Ruth," I whispered, barely able to speak. If I had been fully awake, I may have taken off running. My life pulse threatened to break out of my chest. I knew I had to tell him what my mother-in-law had said to me. "I am your servant. Spread your cloak over your servant for Mother Naomi said you are next-of-kin."

Boaz rubbed his eyes, paused for an eternity, cleared his throat and spoke tenderly, "May you be blessed by the Lord, my daughter; this last instance of your loyalty is better than the first; you have not gone after younger men whether rich or poor. And now, do not be afraid. I will do for you all that you ask, for all the assembly of my people know you are a worthy woman. But now, though it is true I am a near kinsman, there is another kinsman more closely related than I am. Remain the rest of the night with me, daughter." He patted my shoulder. "In the morning when I ask him, if he will do for you as next-of-kin, good, let him do it. If he is unwilling, then, as the Lord lives, I will act as next-of-kin for you. Lie down until morning, yet you must leave before daybreak, before anyone can see a woman spent the night with me." He cleared his throat, and lay back again.

I arose while it was still dark, as I had found it impossible to sleep after everything Boaz said to me. I stood up to go, but Boaz was up and said, "Give me your cloak." Into it, he measured out six measures of barley, tied the cloak, and placed it on my back.

"I am leaving early to attend to business in the city," he said, and he placed his hand firmly on the bundle he had put on my back. It felt as if his hand had patted me, and it pleased me.

I left quickly, while it was only beginning to show signs of light on the rim of the earth. As I hastened on, past the barn onto the next lane, I heard footsteps behind me. I thought perhaps he had followed to make sure I got home safely. When I looked back over my shoulder, I saw the shape of a man approaching and it was not Boaz. At first, I thought nothing of it as it was probably someone getting an early start to his day in the fields. He kept following, and soon walked beside me. "Where were you so early, woman? Did you steal all the barley on your back from the threshing barn of Boaz? It looks heavy. May I relieve you of the burden?" He sneered, accusing me.

I hesitated to answer, as I was a woman alone and

defenseless. I kept walking, picking up my pace almost running.

"Aha, now I know you stole the grain!" He grabbed at my cloak and practically choked me.

"No, no, I am bringing it home as a gift to my poor mother." My mouth was dry and my voice had sounded raspy as I pleaded. "Have mercy. I am a gleaner."

"A foreigner! You have no mother here. You are a common prostitute."

I decided nothing I would say would deter him, so I kept silent and continued to run and walk as quickly as possible toward Naomi's home. He kept pace with me, and I did not know what would happen. I said a silent prayer to Yahweh and asked for protection. Was there any reason Yahweh would keep me from harm? I do not know when the man left me, or how I actually got to our doorstep.

When I arrived at home, Naomi met me eagerly, and said, "How did things go for you, my daughter?" She and I removed my cloak full of grain from my back and set it on the swept dirt floor.

I sat down, weak-kneed, much excited, and full of details, but not of the assailant along the way. I related what Naomi wanted to hear, trying to recall all Boaz had said to me.

"Be still, my daughter, for Boaz will not rest until he settles the matter with the kinsman," Naomi said.

"You know the kinsman, Boaz, but do you know the man he refers to as the nearer kin than him?"

"Yes, I know of him, but not as well. He is a little younger than Boaz, may have a wife, or a woman with whom he plans marriage, but I am not sure of it. If so, he could have you as a second wife. We wait. I do not know much about the man. I do not remember his name."

I did not like to think of being some man's second wife, especially a man I did not know. We ate our morning porridge and I went for water at the well. I brought water inside to wash our dishes. I heated some in a kettle and then washed not only the dishes but wiped our kitchen clean. I did not go to the field to glean barley since Boaz had loaded my back with grain folded into my cloak. Naomi said nothing more and busied herself with household chores.

I was tired as I had not slept past midnight when Boaz had awakened to find me at his feet. I thought dreamily about the man and imagined what life might be with such a good man. In so many ways he was like Elimelech in his decisiveness, kindness, and success as a farmer. I could be happy with him, and Naomi would be cared for in our household as she aged. Boaz was a sturdy man, ageless, but certainly no longer a boy as Mahlon had been when we had married. Sunshine had cast a warm glow from the window where I sat, and I drifted off to sleep, imagining what my life might be like with Boaz, and praying it would not be the other kinsman I didn't know.

11. Boaz

*This is what I have seen to be good: it is fitting to eat and
drink and find enjoyment in all the toil with which
one toils under the sun the few days of the life
God gives for this is our lot.*

Ecclesiastes 5: 18

As I slept on the threshing barn floor, something awakened me with a start. I felt a warm body by my feet and it was not a dream. A fear caused my whole body to prickle. Could one of the servant women try to trick me? I sat up with a start and demanded, "Who are you?"

She answered with a soft shaky voice, "I am Ruth your servant, spread your cloak over your servant, for you are next-of-kin."

I was both shocked and honored. What could I say in response? I said, "May you be blessed by the Lord, my daughter; this last instance of your loyalty to Naomi is better than the first." I told her I was a near kinsman, but another kinsman more closely related should have first preference and I would try to see him soon and ask him if he wanted the property. I didn't want her to leave me, but stay. In my heart, I felt obligated to be honorable in the matter, but I really hoped the man would not want to marry Ruth, because I already cared deeply for her. I said to Ruth, "Leave before the sun is up as it would not be good for anyone to know a woman was here with me all night."

I awakened and filled her cloak with six measures of barley so she would not have to come and glean. I fastened it to her back to make it easier for her to carry. I refreshed myself and went to the city gate and sat down on a stone bench. The next-of-kin, Talmon, came passing by.

"Come sit, I have a bit of business to discuss with you." When he sat down, I continued, "Naomi has come back from the land of Moab where the family lived and prospered during our drought. Elimelech and his sons have all died. She is selling the parcel of land which belonged to our kinsman, Elimelech. So, I am telling you in the presence of those sitting here and the elders. of my people, if you will, redeem it, but if you will not, tell me, for there is no one prior to you, and I come after you."

"I will redeem it!" Talmon said eagerly.

"Good, the day you acquire the fields from the hand of Naomi, you also will acquire Ruth, Mahlon's Moabite widow to maintain the dead man's name on his inheritance."

Upon finding out he would acquire a Moabite widow as his wife with Elimelech's property, the kinsman sat in stunned silence for a moment and then removed his sandal and declared, "I cannot redeem it for myself without damaging my own inheritance. Take my right of redemption for yourself, for I cannot redeem it."

I took his sandal and said to the people surrounding us, "Today you are witnesses I have acquired from Naomi all that belonged to Elimelech and her sons Chilion and Mahlon. I have also acquired Ruth, the widow of Mahlon to be my wife, to maintain the dead man's name on his inheritance in order that the name of the dead may not be cut off from his kindred and from the gate of his native place. Today you are my witnesses."

Then all the men who were at the gate and the elders said, "We are your witnesses."

"It's about time you found a woman before all your sap dries!" One friend exclaimed. Laughter ensued, but I didn't stay to listen.

My feet were as if they had wings as I went back to my home. I wanted to go directly to Ruth with the news, but I stopped at my home, then decided to go to the barley field to see how things were going. Everything looked as it should be. The harvesting servants were busily cutting sheaves in the far reaches of the field. Gleaners were following behind them as usual gathering what was left behind. Before long, the field would be completely done.

I took a deep breath, looked out and did not see Ruth among the women. Of course not, I had given her enough barley to last awhile. Although I could not wait to see her to tell her and Naomi of the news, I was pleased she had taken the day off after what was no doubt a difficult night for her with little sleep.

Naomi's home was swept clean in front as I walked to the door. A decorative pot adorned either side of the doorway. I barely knocked, and Ruth answered with her wide-eyed face inquiring before she spoke any words. "Please come in and sit with us. Naomi and I were about to have tea and honey cakes."

"What did our kinsman say?" Naomi asked. She had posed the question before I was seated with them on the floor mats by the low table.

"The kinsman, Talmon, would not redeem the property and Ruth, as he said it would affect his own inheritance." I left out the part where he had first agreed to the property, but changed his mind when he found out he would get Ruth, a Moabite widow, as wife in the bargain.

Naomi smiled broadly, but Ruth turned her face away shyly, and I saw her cheeks had flushed. Her reaction confirmed what I had hoped; she may have found me desirable despite my age.

"The counsel of men at the gate were witness to the transaction between the kinsman and me, but I wish to register for all time our agreement in the Synagogue."

"Is it necessary? Do I need go with you?" Naomi asked. Naomi had a curved back and she walked stooped over a bit.

"I can handle it with the word of the men who were witnesses this morning."

Ruth sat silently and placed honey cakes on the cloth in front of me, poured some flavorful herbal tea and honey into a colorful ceramic bowl for me to drink.

"Besides the legal business, you women will know more about the wedding details to be handled, so I will put those plans into your capable hands, Naomi."

"I will plan a wedding. Do you and Ruth want a small ceremony with only ourselves in attendance with a rabbi or priest from our local Synagogue? Or shall we have a great celebration and feast with all our friends in attendance? I do not know what I can afford. Certainly not what we did when …"

Naomi stopped speaking and looked aside. She drew a small cloth from her skirts and wiped her face. "I seem to have a bug in my eye," she said.

I could tell she was recalling the weddings of her sons and could not go on talking as emotions came upon her suddenly. I looked at Ruth.

"It does not matter to me, which way we plan," Ruth said. She looked earnestly at Naomi and then at me.

I could have melted when her eyes sought mine. How could I have been so blessed to have her at this time in my life. I sensed she would rather put her past behind her since she had made up her mind to be with Naomi and her family and friends. I did wonder if she believed in Yahweh or still had a faith in Chemosh.

"I will pay for whatever you two women decide to do, whether a large or small celebration. It can be at my home. A happy occasion it will be when I have Ruth as my bride to bring to my home and to cherish forever." I turned toward Ruth and teased, "You will still have me?"

Ruth smiled and nodded.

Naomi then did something I did not expect. She took Ruth's hand and placed it in my hand. I was having strong urgings I had not had in years, and wondered how long it would take before the wedding until I could hold her in my arms and we would be married. It was the custom for marriages to be arranged by parents like a business transaction. What I had was a business deal of sorts. If love happened somewhere along the way so much the better, but it was not the usual basis for marriage.

"I have business to attend to," I said. I kissed Naomi on both cheeks, and did the same for Ruth, whose tender cheeks tasted like sweet honey to me.

I rushed away, but looked back toward the house, hoping I would see Ruth standing in the doorway. She had already stepped inside, so I set my mind on the business at hand. I had grain storage to deal with, carts to be loaded, and a man I would meet who wanted to buy barley from me. Spelt harvest was next. Work never let up during harvest, but I was so very thankful to Yahweh we could now grow crops and have grain to sell and store.

Tomorrow my business would be to go to the Synagogue in Jerusalem to register our betrothal in the record for all time. I thought it would be important for generations to come to seek and find out who their ancestors had been. Before I left, I wondered if the authorities there would need to know the name of Ruth's parents. I hoped not, as while I knew where they lived, I did not have any information as to their names.

The next day, I decided to visit Naomi and Ruth before I left to find out any information I might need. While I stood outside knocking on their door, it suddenly occurred to me Ruth might have returned to my fields after having taken the prior day off from gleaning. Naomi opened the door to me, expressing surprise, "Good day, Boaz, please come in and sit."

I came in, did not sit, and glanced at the kitchen. Ruth was not there. "Is Ruth out in the field again today?"

"Yes, she is supposed to be there, did you not see her?"

"No, I came here first today, as I was planning to go to the Synagogue and record our betrothal and upcoming marriage. I might need to know her father's name." I said, and chuckled. "I have never recorded a betrothal before."

Naomi smiled. "You may simply say she is Mahlon's Moabite widow of the house of Elimelech. It will probably be enough to identify her. I believe her father was named Abelmoab."

"Very well, I had best be on my way before the day runs on as I also want to return home to my fields while it is still daylight."

I walked back to my home where I harnessed a strong donkey to pull a small riding cart to take me to the Synagogue. I could have walked the distance, but thought it would take less time to ride. I fully intended to be back in the field later to see Ruth who had come to glean. It was a bright day, and I was humming as I went. I daydreamed about how my life would be with

Ruth by my side, to share my whole life with her. I hoped it would not take Naomi too long to put together the details for the wedding. She was a dear capable woman, and Ruth was devoted to her and helped her with everything.

I looked forward to a large wedding feast and celebration at my home. We had not had any such merriment in the area in years. I would put Naomi in contact with the best vintner in the area, and the wine would flow freely at our wedding. Of course, at my home, I needed to get my servants ready, especially the cook who knew how to roast a fatted calf. My mind was awash with plans and I hoped Ruth was as excited as I was.

Would we have children? I prayed Yahweh would open Ruth's womb and give us sons and daughters. Ruth had not had a child with Mahlon and I hoped she was not barren. My heart sang, dreaming of holding her in my arms and smelling the sweet scent of her. Would she compare me to Mahlon? He had been young, virile, and inexperienced, so surely there was no parallel. My dreamlike reverie went on and on as the clopping rhythm of the donkey kept progressing on the trail.

Suddenly the donkey reared up and upset the cart with me in it. I had landed on the packed earth, unhurt. I stood, and dusted myself off as best I could and watched helplessly as my frightened donkey ran off, dragging my broken cart. Then I saw it, a big snake slithered near me. I looked around for a stone large enough to kill it, but there were only small pebbles. Sweat beaded on my forehead, while a chill prickled my arms like briars. Standing still, I feared the worst, but knew if I ran it might be fatal as well.

12. Ruth

The human mind plans the way,
but the Lord directs the steps.

Proverbs 16: 9

I was elated as I began my bright sunny day after I had learned Boaz was to be the one who would marry me and redeem Elimelech's property. I had very much dreaded the possibility I would have to marry a man I had never met who could possibly already have another wife. We had plenty of barley, but I was looking forward to a day in the field with Boaz. I dressed and grabbed my basket, kissed Naomi's cheeks and told her, "I am gleaning again today."

She smiled knowingly. "Come home early as we have things to discuss and a wedding to plan."

I nodded, and was out the door. When I got to the field, I saw the harvest crew was now at the far end of the field. Soon there would be nothing left except stubble until the next year. I had a long way to walk before I could glean, but I skipped like a child, very happy I would soon see Boaz.

Shapes of women in the distance reassured me I could join the gleaners. Daydreaming as I went, I failed to notice anything behind me. Suddenly a man crept up from nowhere, seized me around the middle and pulled me roughly to his body. His hardness and anger came to fore in his actions, and I was afraid he would violate me in daylight. He thrust me on the earth among dry scratchy stubble, and dust choked my nose and throat. I yelled out hoarsely, and hoped Boaz was even now looking for me to show up in the field, but then I remembered he had to go to the Synagogue. Why was the man treating me thus? They had all been warned to leave me alone.

I had to think, and do something quickly. "I am diseased! You are welcome to it." I croaked.

He loosened his hold on me a moment. "You are telling me this lie to make me let you go?" He sneered. "I know your kind you, foreign prostitute."

He was not a harvester in the field where I had been gleaning. I realized by his ugly voice he was the same man who had tried to accost me in the morning before daylight after my night on the threshing floor. While he had released his hold on my arms, his body still pinned mine to the earth. With one free hand, I quickly scooped a handful of dirt and flung it at his face. He let out a yelp, and tried to wipe his eyes. In so doing, his body shifted enough for me to pelt him with more dirt, and enabled me to roll free of him. Part of my garment was caught up between his legs and as I forced myself up, it ripped. I ran, leaving my basket behind. I did not know where I was going, but thought it best to get as close to the other women as possible. An older woman, Miriam, who had talked with me before saw me and said, "What happened to you? Did you fall among the stubble?"

"Yes, I fell."

She nodded, knowingly. "You must be more careful." She had a vial of some ointment she applied to my hand which was bleeding. Then she took my hand and led me to the water buckets where she used a cloth to wipe the dirt off of me. "You tore your robe."

"I did. I can mend it." I was so grateful for her help,

but was afraid to reveal the truth of the assailant who caused all of my distress.

"Next time, come when we all do and you will have a safer walk. It is a long way now since the field is almost finished for the season. We won't be doing this field for many more days."

"Is the field owner here today?"

"I have not seen him yet," she replied.

Boaz was not among the men, so I knew he had gone to register our betrothal today. I really wanted to confide in Miriam and tell her everything, like I used to tell Orpah. I missed my friend very much, but was reluctant to make another close friend who could be gone from my life at any time. It may have been foolish, but I did not want to risk the pain again.

At the end of the day, I returned to Naomi who saw my torn garment, but said nothing about it. Had she done so, I would have simply said I fell among the stubble on my way to glean and had torn it. In my sewing basket was a needle and some mending yarn with which I could repair it. While there was still light from the window, I sat down to sew.

Naomi said, "Boaz came by today on his way to Synagogue to record the betrothal. He wanted to know your father's name and how he should enter your information in the book of record. I told him to enter you as Mahlon's widow from the house of Elimelech."

"I am grateful you gave him the information. He was not in the field today, so I was sure he had gone there. A good business man and farmer, he never seems to put anything off for another day." I would not say aloud my thought of how much he reminded me of Elimelech in his ability and sense of duty.

Sewing always calmed my thoughts, so in a way I was thankful I had mending to do. The light was waning as I put in the last stitches to repair the tear. During my stitching, I had let my thoughts wander to what my life would be going forward. Naomi would soon be asking me numerous questions about what I would like to have happen at the wedding, and how soon it would take place. Normally an agreement between parents of the girl and her intended husband, or his parents, would take a year to accomplish. The parents of Boaz were deceased, and I was a widow. Exceptions in the law and social expectations were in order for us so we would not have to wait a full year unless we wished. What would I wear? My hands were deft to sew and make a garment, so I planned on going to market to buy fabric for my wedding dress. I was deep in thought about what colors I might be able to find and what the finished product would look like, when Naomi cleared her throat.

"Ruth, I have baked bread today and we have cheese, dates, and wine. Are you ready for our supper?"

I set my garment aside as I had finished mending it. "Yes, I am hungry and thirsty." I rose and went to help her place the items on our low table where we sat next to it on cushions and ate our supper. It was a welcome treat, as I had suddenly realized how hungry I was after my eventful day. I wondered if we would see Boaz this evening.

"By now, Boaz must surely be home," Naomi said. She dipped bread into her bowl of red wine and had a satisfied look on her face. "He will be too tired to come here tonight."

"I suppose so," I said, but wondered why he had not shown up at the field late when we were all preparing to leave. Something must have caused him to delay. I hoped he had not been beset by robbers. I wondered if today would be the first of many times I might worry about Boaz when he failed to return in a timely manner. Naomi sat next to me nibbling bread. I sipped my wine, lost in my thoughts, then I said, "I would like a small, quiet wedding, which would be less bother for you to plan."

"Ruth," Naomi said my name as if she were about to scold. "Please, it is not like you to think only of yourself. Boaz has never married, is a well-known, respected land owner and farmer. Do you not think he should have a great celebration?"

"I am sorry, I did not mean to belittle him in any way." I felt my face flush with embarrassment.

"You heard him say he would pay for the expense. I think he fully expected we would plan for all of his friends and kin to attend and rejoice with him. It would celebrate not only his marriage, but all the neighbors' joy at our drought being over." Naomi sounded insistent.

I heard her say "his marriage" and wondered if she had completely forgotten I was a part of it. He was the family redeemer, after all, and very important. As a woman, and part of the bargain, I was less important in her eyes. Boaz had looked upon my face, and in his eyes, I had seen admiration and respect. I clung to the thought.

Perhaps now would not be the time to talk with Naomi about what I would wear for the ceremony and other days of the week-long celebration which would surely take place. The safest subject would be where the wedding would occur, so I asked, "Where will our ketubah and wedding be held?"

"We cannot have it here in this small place," she said. "Since he will be taking you to his nice home on his property, I think it would be fitting to have it there."

"I would like it to be so, if Boaz wants to do it." I had already thought there would be no question as to where it would be. "How will we get word out to the people whom we wish to invite? Will it be by carriers of messages, or some other way?"

"Boaz will let us know who to invite, yet it may be the entire neighborhood as he has many friends. Since he is paying for the food, I need also to know about how many we will feed and provide with good wine. I can arrange for it once I know the day of the wedding."

"Do you still have connections from years ago when you lived here?"

"Yes, I know some, have renewed those friendships, and become acquainted with new women and tradesmen in the marketplace since our return here. A butcher I know has the best fatted calves to prepare for the feast." Naomi sounded excited. I was glad she had the wedding to plan, but realized she would probably not consult with me on many details. "And there is the matter of what you will wear."

"Truly, as I want to look my best on our wedding day," I said. "Have you any preference, or may I tell you what I would like?"

"Ruth, your wedding garment should be splendid of linen and silks, and you should wear jewels."

"I would favor a many-colored linen robe and a silken scarf and sash. I could wear the shell necklace my mother gave me."

"You have thought about what you would wear. Shiny gems would be more fitting for a wife of Boaz. Of course, I know your shell necklace is nice, and there will be a whole week to wear different jewelry, but for the wedding day, I would prefer to have something prettier for you. I am glad you have not been so busy gleaning you have not considered such things. I know a woman named Rebekah who sews beautifully. We could have her sew your wedding garments. I shall contact her so she can come here and measure you to sew clothes to fit you."

Naomi was acting in place of my own mother, who I knew would not travel here for the occasion. She had washed her hands of me when I had married Mahlon, a foreigner who did not worship Chemosh. Never mind that my father worshipped Yahweh, and Chemosh in name only to keep peace with my mother.

It was somehow strange to be discussing wedding plans and my dress with Naomi, who was my mother-in-law when Mahlon was alive. My emotions came upon me suddenly, and I looked away. It did not seem so long ago when my mother and I had planned what I would wear when I had married Mahlon. Why was I thinking of Mahlon? In truth, not hearing from Boaz as he had made a trip of some distance made me deeply worried, as I had lost Mahlon when he had traveled.

People who traveled alone were vulnerable, open to robbers and the like. I could not get my mind to think of anything else; what might have happened to him? In a donkey-drawn cart, he should have been able to get the business taken care of and been back while we were all still in his fields at day's end working at the last light. I blurted out to Naomi, "What do you suppose has delayed Boaz?"

Naomi looked at the ceiling as if she might find an answer there, but did not respond. I could see her thoughts were similar to mine as she had lost her son on a trek to get supplies. "We will know by tomorrow," she said.

"Is there anyone in the neighborhood who would make a run to the Synagogue to see if they can find out?"

"No, it is dark. No one would want to be out now. We will trust Yahweh he is only delayed because he found someone he has not seen recently and spent the day visiting."

Her idea did not hold true to what I knew of Boaz. He set about doing something and got it accomplished as soon as he could before he set about doing anything else. He would not have whiled away his time for a casual visit with an old friend. If he had, I realized I probably did not know as much about him as I thought.

I worried, and sleep would not come as I lay on my comfortable woolen mat with my life pulse pounding relentlessly in my breast.

13. Boaz

The mind of the wise makes their speech judicious,
and adds persuasiveness to their lips.
Pleasant words are like honeycomb, sweetness
to the soul and health to the body.

Proverbs 16: 23-24

We were at an impasse. The snake was still coiled as if to strike, but did not move, and I was still. His beady dark eyes stared at me and never blinked. I do not know how long I stood fearing the snake would strike, but not wanting to run as then surely it would. Then I heard wagon wheels on the road in the distance.

Rabbi Matteaus came up in his oxen yoked cart as I stood there helplessly looking for a stone to kill the snake, which was not as large as it first appeared when I lay on the ground. The sound must have scared the snake away as he slunk off into the brush beside the road. "God's good day to you, Rabbi Matteaus," I said. "I am very happy to see you come along."

"Why are you standing in the middle of the road when a man wants to proceed on his journey?" Matteaus said, with a note of humor in his voice.

"When a snake startled him, my donkey reared up and ran away with my donkey cart, left me where I had fallen in the dirt. The snake has gone into the brush now."

"A snake may cause all sorts of trouble. The first scroll says one of them was Adam's downfall," Matteaus said. "Where were you planning to go? I could give you a lift if you wish."

As I climbed in beside him on the bench where he was sitting directing the oxen, I said, "My old scroll-quoting rabbi, I would be ever so grateful for a ride. I need to get to the Synagogue to do some important business."

"May I ask what important business you are conducting in the middle of your barley harvest?'

"I am the kinsman redeemer for Elimelech's widow Naomi, who has returned from Moab with only a daughter-in-law who is also a widow. I want to register the property correctly."

"News has it you also are getting the young daughter-in-law as your wife. Will you register a betrothal as well?"

"Yes, I am to be wedded to Mahlon's widow Ruth."

Rabbi Matteaus sat quietly for a moment before he remarked, "Will she be worshipping Chemosh like her people? If so, you may have bought yourself a handful of trouble."

I was silent, trying to remember exactly what Naomi had told me about Ruth's loyalties, but since I could not recall what she had said, I kept it to myself. If he was right, I could possibly have difficulties in our relationship, particularly if we were to have a son who I would insist be circumcised. I thought Naomi had told me Ruth would worship our God, but I decided to change the subject. "Barley harvest is going well. My largest field will probably be finished with harvesting today or tomorrow."

"Are you not usually there to oversee it day after day? I have heard you even sleep on the threshing room floor some nights."

I laughed, "The rumor is true; some nights I cannot get my bones to move on home so I do sleep there."

"The lunatic, Dodopulus, said a woman was seen leaving the threshing barn before dawn one day. No one believes Dodopulus, but I wondered if you knew of it."

"Ha! Why wouldn't a man have some woman spend a cool night there to warm him?" I chuckled, "How many has he seen? One? More? In truth, no woman would want to bed down with a man on the floor."

"Dodopulus has no sense," Rabbi Matteaus said, chuckling.

Our conversation went on to politics and weather, and harvests until the Synagogue came into view. "What do I see up ahead?" Rabbi Matteaus said.

I burst out laughing. As if my donkey knew where I was going, he and the mangled cart were in the middle of the road on the way to the Synagogue. He was lying down as best he could. I got out of the ox cart to see my donkey. "His leg is injured," I said as I inspected the poor beast.

"Continue to ride with me, Boaz. We will find help for you in town."

I was already untangling the reins and harness from my donkey and murmuring reassuringly to him. I pushed the cart off of the road as I thought there was no way I could repair it here. Rabbi Matteaus patiently waited for me to answer him, but did not come down to help me. In truth, there was nothing he could do. I encouraged my donkey to stand on all fours, but he balked and lay back down, imploring me with his large eyes to leave him be. I gently got him off of the road so he would not be in the way. "I suppose I must leave the beast here," I said, and climbed up beside Rabbi Matteaus.

"A bad start for the day, eh Boaz? I will get you to Synagogue, but I have other business which will not wait, so I must leave you there to find your way back to your home."

"I understand, and I appreciate you giving me a ride as you have done. While my day has not gone as planned, it has been my good fortune to have your help. Earlier, when we were talking about my upcoming wedding, I meant to ask if you would be willing to perform the rite of marriage for me and my bride."

"It will depend upon the date, of course, but I will be honored to serve as the officiant at your wedding. For you, my friend, it has been a long time coming, and I urge you not to wait very long. You may still have sons even at your age. Who knows where the favor of Yahweh will take us?"

"I am so grateful and will be letting you know when the ceremony will take place. I have left the details up to Naomi, but I will be excited to tell her of your agreement to officiate as Rabbi."

Synagogue was modest in appearance, both outside and in its interior which had room for participants to spread mats on the floor, as well as stone benches which lined the walls where people could sit. There was a section in the back for the women with benches as well. Inside the cool, almost dark interior, I looked for the offices of those in authority. When I approached the door it was closed, so I knocked. No one answered. I stood waiting patiently for what seemed like an eternity. Finally, a small gray-bearded man wearing a faded gray robe opened the door.

The side-locks on his wizened face bobbed as he looked up at me with rheumy hazel eyes, and asked, "What is your business here today?"

"I am Boaz of Bethlehem, and wish to register a property agreement between Elimelech's widow, Naomi, and myself. It will include a marriage to her daughter-in-law."

He nodded and motioned for me to enter his office. Therein, he pulled down a scroll from a shelf and spread it on the polished wood table. "Here is a quill, and here is carbon for you to write what you will on this page."

Still standing, as I had not been invited to sit, I took the quill and dipped it to write on the parchment. I wrote it all, the property, the agreement to take Ruth, a widow, as my wife, and then signed my name.

The old man nodded, and waited for me to say something or add anything more, to which I wrote it was Tishri when I had signed the document. He waited to roll up the scroll, lest the ink smear. "The Lord's good day to you, Boaz," he said as he watched me leave his office. I put some shekels in the treasury on my way out. I was elated, and could not wait to go back to tell Naomi and Ruth our registration was completed and now in the official record.

In the bright sunshine of the day, out on the street, I looked for anyone I might know, or anyone at all. Some women, with little children in tow, headed for the market street. I walked there as well, and stopped at a stand selling fruit. I was hungry and bought figs and a ripe plum. I was hoping for someone selling a juice drink and found a vintner who had grape juice as well as wine. I quenched my thirst with a hearty goblet of wine. Thus invigorated, set about the business of going back to my donkey who was no doubt still down the road. I passed a well, and grabbed a bucket someone had left, filled it with water, drank some myself and hurried to my donkey to slake his thirst.

I walked fast, thinking I would have to walk back to Bethlehem. When I approached my donkey, a young boy was sitting next to him. "God's good day, young man, thank you for keeping my donkey company while I did business in town."

"It is my donkey," the boy said, as he stood to greet me. "My name is Silas."

"I am Boaz," I said. "Why do you think it is your donkey?"

"My donkey died, and I think Yahweh has provided me with another, but this one is injured."

"I am sorry your donkey is dead, but what you see here is my donkey. He was pulling a cart to carry me to the Synagogue when a snake caused him to run away, dumping me on the ground, hurting himself, and ruining my cart."

"Why did you not stay with him to take care of him, but left him here to die?"

"I had business to attend." I put the bucket of water next to my donkey, and I helped him stand so he could drink. "Do you need any water," I asked.

The boy bent to the bucket and slurped water like an animal. Then he splashed water on his face. "I needed water." His clothes were old, dirty, almost rags, and his hands were soiled, his hair an unruly black mop.

I had compassion for him, and wished my cart was not sitting there in disrepair, as I would have offered him a ride anywhere he wanted to go. I went to inspect the cart and set it up on its wheels. It was somewhat broken, but if I had the right tools I could repair it. "Where is your mother?" I asked. I would not ask about a father as sometimes these poor children did not even know him.

"She's busy at home." Silas continued to keep a hand on my donkey. In different circumstances, I would have given the boy a donkey. At the moment, mine was almost useless to me and I still did not know how I would set things right and be able to go home.

"Do you know anyone in town who could help us with the cart and donkey? I can walk there quickly if you would remain here to watch the cart and donkey for me."

He shook his head, as if to say no, but suddenly brightened. "I know a man in town who repairs all kinds of things. His name is Simon."

"Where will I find him?"

"I will go with you. My lame donkey is not going anywhere."

With Silas leading the way, we came to a man who had a forge and was busy making something he had to weld. "Simon!" Silas yelled. "Will you help me?"

Simon kept working as he could not put down the project he worked on, but had to stay at it until it was either to a certain point or finished. At last he turned to us and looked surprised. He probably did not often see a raggedy-dressed boy with a man such as me at his business. "What would you like me to build?" He looked at me and ignored Silas.

"I do not know if you can help. I have a cart needing repair."

"Where is it?" He looked beyond me thinking I had brought it with me.

"It isn't here, but failed me down the road as I came here. I will need help getting it to you so you can decide whether or not you can do the job."

"I do not have such a service." He pulled the leather protection back on and bent back over the lance he was working on.

Silas looked up at me undaunted. "I am strong. You and I will pull it here."

"I should have suggested it in the first place." I grabbed the boy's hand and started running back down the road. He chortled as we ran, trying to keep pace with me. I let go his hand so he could run freely.

It took more time than I thought I had to get to the cart, make sure the donkey had another drink, and pull the cart toward the man's shop in town. When we got there, Simon had finished his work and sat with a bowl of wine cupped in his hands. "You found a way to get it here." He made no attempt to get up and look at my cart which I had left respectably near, but not inside.

"Would you please take a look and let me know if you think you can repair the cart?" I asked. "I can pay whatever fair price you set."

"I can repair anything," he said, still sitting and resting. He eyed the boy dressed in rags.

"The boy is not mine, nor my servant," I said.

"I see," Simon said. "I have seen the boy before. He is a beggar."

With what appeared to be considerable effort, Simon got up and went to the cart. He did not ask a fee and started looking at the wheels and underpinnings of it, handled a broken slat, nodded and calculated how much it would take to make it usable again.

I stood by and watched the man begin to work wonders with what I had thought was destined to be thrown away. It took him a while.

"Good as new," Simon said. I paid him more than he asked.

"Now we will go get my donkey," Silas said.

I berated myself for not looking into the possibility of replacing the donkey before the evening. As I looked toward the rim of the earth, I could see the sun was getting ready to depart. I would not be home before nightfall and see Ruth today.

Did I dare try to walk home in the dark? And what about the boy, would he insist on going with me, or would he be stubborn and stay with the donkey?

I heard the faint voice of a woman calling in the distance, "Silas, where are you? Come home. Come now, or I will come get you." The last words she uttered sounded angry.

Silas pretended not to hear, and I had not decided whether to stay or go.

"Why don't you go home now. I appreciated your help." I reached into my money pouch and brought out a few coins which I put in his eager grimy hand.

"I cannot go without my donkey," Silas sounded as if he would cry.

"We talked about the donkey. You know it belongs to me," I said. I was walking rapidly toward my donkey pulling my repaired cart. The boy had his hand on it and kept up with me, but said nothing. Upon looking at the rim of the earth I was disheartened my daylight was slipping away at the fourth watch. Ever since Yahweh had answered my prayers to finally end the drought, I had been too busy to think of asking anything of the Lord, or thanking him. I could not keep up the pace any longer, so I stopped walking. I knelt there beside the road and pleaded, "Yahweh, I thank you for helping me find a man who would repair my cart, and even for Rabbi Matteaus getting me to the Synagogue, and now I implore you to help me find a way to get home tonight."

Silas looked at me as if to ask a question, but said nothing. He then knelt beside me and said, "Is Yahweh real? Have you ever seen him? If he is real, why is my mother poor and makes me beg?"

I was not experienced in answering questions children would ask. I silently prayed to Yahweh for an answer to reply to the tender boy. I had grown fond of the boy and his innocent, helpful ways. I watched disheartened as the light dipped below the rim of the earth. Now, I was sure I would be lying on the ground to sleep near my donkey until daylight would clear my head as to whether I would walk the distance home, or back into the town to purchase another donkey.

"You should go home, Silas. Your mother will worry." I patted his shoulder and hoped he would heed my words, so I could continue on my way home.

"My mother will beat me. I made no money today, and she will tell me I am lazy. She will never believe I found my donkey alive, especially since I will not be able to take it home with a leg injury."

"You have the coins I gave you. Make your own decision. It will be so dark soon the decision will have to be to stay and sleep on the ground."

"It would not be the first time I slept on the ground," Silas said, bitterly.

I pulled my extra cloak from the cart and spread it on the ground. Then I lay the one I had worn next to it. The water in the bucket was low by now and grimy so I decided not to try to wash my hands and face, but simply lay down on my cloak. While I did not invite the boy to lay down on my extra cloak, he tentatively sat there as if waiting for me to say something. I closed my eyes as I was very tired and it felt good to stretch out after a day when much had gone wrong, but some things had gone well. Night birds cooing in the distance kept me awake for a time, but I must have drifted off to sleep.

When I awakened, it was not yet daylight, the first watch. The boy was curled up on my extra cloak. His eyelids rimmed with long dark lashes were the picture of innocence and I thought how if I had married when I was younger, I would likely have a child about his age. I wondered if I ought to wake him, or let him sleep. I looked where my donkey was. He had risen on all fours. I was not sure how much healing could have taken place in only a day. He was tethered, but walked a couple of paces. I went to inspect his leg and saw the swelling had gone down and only a scrape remained.

"Silas, get up," I said.

He sat up quickly and looked around with a frightened appearance. "What happened?"

"Look at your donkey," I said.

"Oh," he exclaimed, rushing over to the donkey and laying his head on his muzzle. "Yahweh, does live. He made my donkey well."

I could not take the boy with me without causing

his mother to be worried, no matter how bad a mother he said she was. I harnessed the donkey to the cart and tried him a few steps pulling it. He did not limp, but did not walk very fast. I made a decision without thinking any further. The cart was not large, but the boy would fit. "Come inside the cart, Silas," I said.

He climbed in and poked his head out as we rode. "Aww, are we going back into the town? I do not want to go home."

We went as far as Simon's forge and shop. He was already up and working as we approached, and heard us, but did not look up until I stopped there. "God's good day to you, Simon."

"I see the cart is holding up well," he said. "What other jobs do you have for me."

"It is not a job, but I need some information. Do you know where the mother of the beggar boy who is with me lives?"

"Do not get yourself into trouble with such a woman. She makes her money from men, uh, on her back."

"I do not want her services, only to let her know where her son has been and to bring him safely home. My donkey can make the trip now after a day and night's rest; I need to get back to Bethlehem and see to my barley harvest without delay."

"Leave him here. My wife will feed him, and he will be able to get himself home. It is best you do not see his homecoming."

Silas thrust out his chin and said, "No, I am going with you and my donkey."

I didn't know what to do to get the boy out of the cart, and said, "Are you not hungry? Simon's wife will give you breakfast."

"No, no," he wailed, "I want to go with you to your house, because you have my donkey."

"Simon, do you know anyone who would like to sell me a donkey." I was seldom bested by any man, but the boy had me in a quandary.

"No, but my brother has a horse he wants to sell. It's old, but it might take the place of a donkey. Jessup lives down this road." He gestured. "Now I must get to work. It has been good to make your acquaintance."

As I was leading the cart down the road, I heard a woman calling loudly from Simon's house. "Are you bringing your company in to eat? The food will not stay warm forever."

Simon stepped out and waved for us to return. I was hungry and knew the boy was as well. We sat in mats around a low table and ate eggs, bread, and some fruit concoction. The boy had a glass of goat milk, and I had wine and water with Simon and his wife. She was a plump middle-aged woman and smiled the whole time. As we said our good-byes and Simon walked to his shop, he said in a low voice, "She is barren, and will feed any child. Maybe I will have the boy over more to eat as he looks too thin."

Simon's brother Jessup was stooped over, and gray hair peeked out of his head wrap. The brown horse had a gray muzzle and swayed back to match its owner. I had ridden before, and asked if I might try to ride it. "You may, the old horse will serve you well. How far do you want to take him?"

"To Bethlehem," I said. "Would he make it?"

"There and back again a few times," Jessup bragged. "Served me well, pulling my wagon, and has a lot of life in him."

I spoke with Jessup enough to agree on a price, and decided to hurry on, as the day was in full sun.

Silas had been out of the cart, at my elbow, interested in my bargaining. I said, "Sit at the cart's driving seat, hold the reins as I was doing before. You watched me the whole way, so you know how. I would like for you to take the donkey and cart back into town now."

"Are we going to my town or yours?" He looked at me intently as I mounted the horse which had only a rope around its neck and a blanket on its back.

"We go as far as Simon's place."

Silas nodded, eyed me as if to question, and began to slap the reins gently to move the donkey cart forward. I rode beside him, hoping my plan would work.

14. Ruth

Be still and know that I am God!
I am exalted among the nations.
I am exalted in the earth.

Psalm 46: 10

I awakened in the morning feeling uneasy, and unrested. Of course, after dark last night, I had not expected Boaz to knock on our door and ease our minds. Naomi was already heating water to make tea, and cook breakfast porridge. She ground the seeds enough to cook and added honey to sweeten it. It was a comfort to wake up and see her doing the normal household tasks. I dressed, washed my face and hands in the basin, and kept hoping for a knock on the door which would reassure me Boaz was indeed well after his trip to Synagogue.

After I finished eating, I grabbed a cloth basket to take to the field to glean. What else could I do this day except sit here and wait and worry.

"Are you gleaning today?" Naomi asked.

"Yes, I am. The harvest is almost done, but there are still heads of barley to be gathered. I wish to go when the other women are walking there as I have made some good friends among them."

Naomi and I kissed cheeks and I left. There were some clouds in the sky which formed a beautiful array of color as the morning sun rose upon us. It did not look as if it would rain and ruin the final days of the ripened sheaves. My mind would not rest for worrying about Boaz. A group of women of different ages and colors of robes were ahead of me as I hurried to meet with them at the edge of the field. Row after row tan stubble stood where there had been waving stalks of grain on those first days I gleaned in the field.

"Ruth, I am happy you are coming again today,"

Miriam called to me, as she slowed her pace until I caught up with her.

"I wonder whether Boaz will be here today," I said.

"He is always in the field unless he has business elsewhere," Miriam said, and looked at me curiously. "You are fond of the man."

"Boaz is a kinsman to Naomi and has been kind to me." I was not ready to tell Miriam we were to be married, and how worried I was about him. What if he had been killed or maimed on his trip yesterday? I wanted to stop thinking about Boaz, but I could not, and I peered into the distance of the field.

"Some have said he is to own Elimelech's property." She paused and looked at me as if to ask a question.

Miriam was my friend now, even though I had not grown up with her as I had Orpah, and I made the decision to confide in her. "I was part of the property belonging to Naomi and Elimelech, and as you probably heard from some wives of men who witnessed the agreement, as kinsman redeemer he also has acquired me."

She stopped walking. The other women were already ahead of us so could not hear us talking. Miriam grasped my arm and faced me with a smile. "I am happy for you. It must be so hard to be a widow at a young age seeing to the care of your mother-in-law in a strange country. Boaz is a good man who will take care of both of you."

I am not usually given to emotions, but her

observation brought tears of joy to my eyes. I truly had a friend. I dropped my cloth basket and faced her, kissed both her cheeks, and said, "Miriam, I am so happy to have you as my friend."

"And I am glad to be your friend." Miriam patted my arm and we hurried to catch up with the other women.

We were gleaning the dropped heads the men had left. I kept looking around, hoping to see Boaz. I wondered if he had returned, whether he had accomplished what he set out to do, and mostly if he was well. The sun had already arisen in the blue sky. My worry grew and made my insides ache.

I heard a commotion as a man came to the field, riding a dark brownish horse. He sat tall on its back and as he neared, I saw it was none other than Boaz. My inside fluttering increased at the sight and I wondered whether he had always had the horse. If he had, why had I never seen him on it. He alit with the help of one of the workers, and looked toward the field, which was nearly all harvested. It took a lot of restraint of my impulses to stay with Miriam and the gleaning women as I had many questions for him.

At midday, I sat on a bundle of sheaves with Miriam and we ate bread which we had with water from the common buckets in the field. Boaz had not come near me, and I was deeply concerned. Had something gone awry with the signing of the property agreement at the Synagogue? Naomi had said he was taking a donkey and small cart on the trip. He must have changed his mind.

While Miriam and I ate and talked, I gave little heed to anything else. I was hurt Boaz had not sought me, but went about his work instead. Someone had led the horse away from the field, so I was surprised when a shadow darkened my hands. "God's good day, Ruth and Miriam," Boaz said. "It is a pity you only have water. We must soon celebrate with fine wine as the harvest is nearly finished for this year."

I was so startled I almost slid off the sheaves where we sat. "Boaz, you have returned," I said.

He patted his right arm with his left hand. "I am really here at last."

"Why did you take so long to come home?" Although I had not intended to do so, I had raised my voice and it almost seemed like a scold.

"Many reasons. May I save the details for both you and Naomi as we have our meal tonight with her. I stopped to see her on my way here and she said I must come this evening as we have much to discuss."

I wanted to kiss his cheeks, hug him, and tell him how worried I had been, yet I sat as serenely as I could and simply nodded my head. It was enough to know he was alive and well.

"Where did they take the horse your rode? I never recall seeing you on a horse before," Miriam said.

"Never rode it before the trek back from Synagogue; I did not have such a horse, and he is part of a long story." Boaz moved on, calling instructions to some of the workers, as they loaded the last sheaves onto wagons to go to the threshing barn. "Stop," he yelled to someone overloading one of the wagons. In a softer voice, looking directly at me, he said, "Work to be done. I must leave you two and be with my men."

I brushed some crumbs from my dress as I stood with Miriam, and we went to continue gleaning where the last sheaves had been cut down and hauled away. Some women had already left with their full baskets. My cloth bundle was about to burst, but I went along with Miriam who still had room in her basket. Sunshine heated the field and I felt the warmth through the soles of my worn sandals. Miriam sighed, and said, "Unless I go to a different field, I think I have gleaned more than enough for a season."

We waved to each other as we parted to go down the same road in opposite directions toward our homes. I hurried, anxious to hear what Naomi would have to say, and whether she knew any more than I did about why Boaz had not come home directly from the Synagogue.

Naomi bent over the kettle on the open hearth as she stirred a delicious smelling stew. I saw fresh bread on the table cooling. "Ruth, good news, Boaz has returned, or maybe you saw him in his fields today."

"He did come before midday, but I did not speak much with him because he was busy managing the last of the harvest, as wagons were loading sheaves to take to the threshing barn. I suppose he came here as he said you had asked him to eat with us tonight."

After I put my basket of grain heads to one side to thresh out the seeds later, I went to the basin of water and washed my grimy face and hands. I looked at my garment and decided it was good enough.

"Change out of your field clothes, Ruth," Naomi advised, "You want to look your best for Boaz who has been working hard all day."

Not any longer or harder than me, I thought, but kept it to myself. Always the dutiful daughter-in-law, I removed my soiled robe, and put on a fresh long tunic and bright yellow sash. I set out cups for wine, big bowls for our stew and a woven basket for bread. I wanted to ask Naomi if she knew the reason he had been detained, but since she did not say anything, I decided to wait for Boaz to tell us what had happened.

It was almost dark when he came, and I opened the door for him to come inside. "Boaz, how nice you could come tonight after a long day in the field," I said.

He looked directly into my eyes and said, "I could not do otherwise after keeping you wondering what might have caused me to be a whole day late coming home from a short trip to the Synagogue."

"I worried," I said softly, and could not divert my eyes from his. He said a lot without speaking.

"Come in and sit before the stew is cold and spoiled," Naomi said.

We sat down. "The property is recorded and all is well." Boaz beamed. Naomi poured wine for us. "To life, to health," we three said. We sopped chunks of bread in the stew to dip and chew, while Boaz began to tell his tale of many reasons he was late, the first of which was a snake which caused the ruin of his cart and hurt his donkey before he arrived there.

"Yahweh brought some good out of it. Rabbi Matteaus and his ox cart were going my way and gave me a lift to the Synagogue. He has agreed to perform the rites for our Ketubah and wedding when we have the ceremony at my home," Boaz said.

"One thing I will not have to think about," Naomi said, as she sipped some wine.

I was eager to hear more, as I was wondering what happened to the cart, and donkey, and how he had come back with a horse instead. Had it taken so long to trade an injured donkey and broken cart for an old horse? He would not have left a helpless donkey to fend for itself. I knew there had to be more to his list of reasons he was late. Had he found another woman? I thought not, but did not know very much about him before I had come to Bethlehem.

"We will have the wedding celebration at your place," Naomi said. "Do you have a fatted calf and lambs to roast for the feast, or shall I buy them from the butcher? The finest wine must be procured, and all manner of vegetables and sweet fruits. Bread should be baked daily and, I forgot to ask you, Boaz, who are we inviting besides ourselves? Will it be all the neighbors and relatives? How many will we need to prepare for?"

Boaz sat as if deep in thought, sipping his wine. "Are there more questions?" He had a bemused look on his face.

"Do you have a clothier who will sew for you a fine garment to wear? And where are there enough tables on which we can set the food each day?" Naomi asked.

"I do know a man whose wife and her workers make wedding garments for both men and women. I will hire him to make Ruth's as well as my garment, if it is your desire. As to the rest of it, my servants will help with the feast, and I can add more to my staff for our celebration." He sounded excited.

I did not ask if Naomi had already asked her acquaintance Rebekah to make my wedding garment. I sat and listened quietly as during none of the plans they discussed had they consulted me or included me. As I realized Naomi would be living with us when we were married, I wondered how many other details in my life would be decided without my having any involvement in it at all. I supposed I would always be the obedient daughter-in-law. Yet, while my thoughts had caused me to be sad, I remembered his eyes speaking deeply to mine as I had welcomed him at the door earlier.

"I must be going home now. We will talk much more in the days ahead." Boaz kissed our cheeks and left almost abruptly. Had I been too silent? Were there other reasons he had left so quickly?

15. Boaz

For I was hungry and you gave me something to eat, I was thirsty and you gave me something to drink, I was a stranger and you welcomed me.

Matthew 25; 35

Once I was back in my home after my evening with Naomi and Ruth, I shook my head at the enormity of the plans Naomi was handling for our celebration. Whenever the wedding was behind us, I had the joyful thought I would forever after have Ruth in my bed during the night. A soft bed of wool and cotton with many pillows for her, much different from the first night she pleaded her case for her and Naomi for me to redeem them while lying on the cold threshing barn floor. I smiled, thinking of her bravery, loyalty and sweetness.

Ruth had been tired and quiet during our meal this evening. Of course, Naomi had not given either of us leave to talk as she went on about wedding plans. What would a man such as me know about weddings? It was best for me to say nothing. I was glad harvest in my field was done, as it would give Ruth time to rest. I lay on my bed making my own plans. Ruth had not had children with Mahlon, and I wondered if there was a reason her womb had not given a child. Yahweh was good, and would provide. I was sure of it. How long had it taken for the drought to lift? Ruth had chosen to come with Naomi for a reason which might not be known for generations. We would be blessed; I was sure of it.

I needed to contact a builder to add rooms to my modest house. It was large enough, but I wanted Naomi to have her room away from the rooms Ruth and I would have. I drifted to sleep, thinking of all of it, and trying not to remember my difficulties when I had gone to the Synagogue. I silently prayed Silas had not tried to follow me, but had gone to his mother as I had instructed him. Had the woman been mean or kind, happy to have her son come home? Silas had usually survived on his own during the day while begging coins to bring home to her. I pleaded for sleep to come, as I wanted to stop thinking of things I could not change.

Days passed. I spoke with a builder named Shad who agreed to build the addition to my home. It would involve a stairway to the roof where the new rooms would be constructed. I gave him money to buy materials and he started building within a few days. My servants stood waiting for me to instruct them as I wanted them to do their work, not bothering the builder unless he asked for their help. I said, "Soon there will be a wedding here as I am marrying the Moabite widow named Ruth. She will be bringing her mother-in-law, Naomi with her, which is why I am having the rooms built. Even before the wedding celebration feast happens, I am asking all of you to be here to do much of the work. Cook, you are skilled at roasting meats, so you will be in charge of the fatted calf and lambs. Your wife Sarai who bakes bread will be baking fresh loaves every day for my guests. It may be too much for Sarai, as I know her leg bothers her, so I will have another baker help. Does anyone have a question?"

"How soon will it be?" A young servant asked.

"Soon, but I do not have a day it will happen yet as

much needs to be done to prepare." I dismissed them with a wave of my hand and they all went back to work with pleasant expressions on their faces.

+++

The threshing barn had neatly piled sheaves, and my men were threshing barley to store in stone and crockery bins. I already had orders of grain to be placed on ox carts and shipped. Some grain was put into sacks which would be sold locally and ground into flour for baking. It was going well as I had expected. Men were calling to each other good-naturedly and a few of them chanted little songs of praise to Yahweh. The atmosphere seemed to foretell of good days to come. I joined in the pulling of choice ears of barley to place in bins. A certain number of the choice ears already in stone containers would be loaded to go to the Temple as a tithe from my harvest. Yahweh had blessed me abundantly. I found myself humming a praise to our creator. "Blessings and honor and praise to you Most High God. For you have looked with favor upon us."

While I remained in a happy state of mind, I failed to see the boy come to the threshing barn. Outside the entrance I heard a commotion, then a man yelled, "Boy, do not come in here. Can you not see there is grain being worked and stored?"

I looked up to see Silas there, with his chin thrust out defiantly, "I am here to see the big man, Boaz."

Surprised, I started to chuckle, and walked toward him. "When did you come, and why are you here in my threshing barn."

"They said you would be here. I brought your cart back to you, as I did not buy it, and my mother told me I had to return it to the man I had taken it from. She thought I stole it."

"Did she know how far you had to go from home to give it back?"

"Um, I did not tell her." He ducked his head a little. "But I did not lie." Silas said.

"How and when do you plan to go back home and explain everything to her? Do you still have the donkey, and is he completely healed?"

"Yes, my donkey is here with your cart. His leg is well, I think."

He had not answered my first question. I saw his clothing was the same it had been, and he looked thinner, his cheek bones were sharp. Some of the men had stopped working to watch the interchange between the boy and me. "Get back to work, all of you. The boy is no concern of yours." Before nightfall, news of my odd little visitor would be all over the community.

"Silas, come with me, and we will have a look at your donkey and cart." Outside, as expected, the donkey was harnessed to the cart and made a short braying noise when we walked up to him. I petted his neck as I had always done in the past, and he nodded his head as if approving of the gesture. "We will both get on the cart and ride to my home, which is not far." We climbed up and headed for my place. The barn work would continue without me.

I stopped at my well and drew some water for the donkey to drink, after first dipping in with the handled cup to give the boy a drink. We went to my house where the builder was starting to stack supplies for his work which would begin the next day. I waved to Shad who came to talk with me. "Who have you here?" Shad asked good-naturedly.

"His name is Silas, and he lives in the town near the Synagogue. He was returning a cart I left there." It was the easiest way to explain the young unkempt boy.

I left him outside and went in to Cook and Sarai. "I have a hungry young man with me who could use some bread with honey," I said. "His name is Silas, and he has made a long trip today."

"Bring him to the kitchen," Sarai said. "I will feed him."

She did not run away at the sight of the boy, but told him to sit on the floor, and brought a small basin of water in which she made him wash his hands and face. Then she gave him goat milk, bread with honey, some cheese, dates and figs. I left him there in her care as I knew she would probably also find some clean clothing for him to wear. She was kind, a grandmother who had raised a family.

Silas looked at me, almost afraid to say anything, and quietly said, "You are good to me."

"Stay here, Silas, I am going back to the threshing barn as there is much work to do," I said. I didn't explain anything further to Sarai and Cook about the boy. They had work to do, and he had his hands and mouth busy with food.

When I started for home after my barn work, I decided to stop by Naomi's house, as I wanted to see Ruth, and reassure myself she was doing well today. She answered the door, smiling. "I am happy to see you," she said. "I heard you had a young boy at the threshing barn today."

"Yes," I said, chuckling. "The boy is part of the many events which took place to delay me coming home. Do you want to hear it all now?"

She nodded, and I came inside to greet both her and Naomi. Naomi insisted I have watered wine and honey cakes. I retold the events concerning Silas as briefly as I could, and all the other details about the cart, the donkey, and the horse. Naomi asked, "Why has the boy come here?"

"I am not sure about all the reasons, but he says his mother told him to return the cart to me. I left the very hungry boy in my kitchen under the care of Sarai, who was feeding him. Boys his age are always hungry."

After a short visit in which I declined another invitation from Naomi to stay for evening meal, I returned home. The donkey was tethered and had water, and the cart was sitting apart and unattended. Upon entering the kitchen to see how Silas had fared under

Sarai's care, I saw him lying asleep on the mat where I had left him eating earlier in the day. Cook was getting our supper ready, and Sarai was bustling around doing other kitchen chores. She saw me and asked, "What do you want to do about the boy. He told me he does not want to go home as his mother beats him almost every day. He is so small." I heard sympathy in her voice.

"What should I do with him?" I opened my hands as if to implore an answer from them.

Cook came back into the room and stood by Sarai. "If you do not want to send him home today, we can put him in the extra room in our house for the night." Their dwelling was on my property, so he would not be far away.

"I will think about it," I said. I saw the boy stirring on the sleep mat on the floor. He stretched and yawned. "Silas, are you awake? Do you think it is about time for you to be going home?"

"It is too dark soon," he said. "May I sleep here on the floor?"

"Will your mother be expecting you?" I knelt beside him and ruffled his unruly, oily hair.

"She will not care," he said. There was no bitterness or emotion in his voice.

I looked at Cook and Sarai, and hoped they would repeat the offer they had made to me, but they waited for me to speak. "The kind woman who fed you and her husband, Cook, have offered to have you stay with them tonight. What would you think of that?"

He sat up suddenly, "I must go out."

I realized, the boy had food and water and needed to relieve himself. I hoped he would choose a place not too close to the house. I talked with Cook and Sarai, who said if the boy needed more time here they would allow him to stay with them longer than tonight, as they had a room for him. I breathed a sigh of relief when Silas returned and said, "My donkey is happy here."

Suddenly loud arguments erupted near the animal pens. "What now?" I rushed out, wondering what else had happened to create a disturbance for me. And then I remembered the nag I had ridden home as I ran out.

16. Ruth

A capable wife who can find?
She is more precious than jewels.

Proverbs 31: 10

At Naomi's insistence, I went to the clothier Boaz had recommended who could make my wedding garments. When we came in, we met Shnayder, and his wife, Shpilke, the owners. She was brown skinned, with dark braided hair, and narrow gray eyes, and he looked a bit older with white in his beard and at his temples. The shop was small, and many kinds of colorful fabrics hung from hooks on the wall. Some stacks of material were folded and piled on the floors by the wall. I had never seen so many colors and types of fabrics. Two women were sitting and sewing in the sunlight which shone in the windows. They kept at their work after they saw us come in to be greeted by Shpilke and her husband. Naomi told them about the upcoming wedding, and the need for at least three different garments for me to wear during the days prior to the wedding while celebrations were going on. Lastly, she had me describe what I would like for my wedding day attire to be. I tried to think clearly, and all I could think about was the dress I had worn when Mahlon and I had married. I started to describe it, but stopped myself, remembering Boaz wanted me to wear something finer, perhaps linen or silk. Linen was usually not worn by any except priests and royalty, so I did not think any of my garments would be made from it.

Naomi was delighted I had chosen a red silken sash for my ivory white outer robe of shimmering cotton fabric. Both Shnayder and Shpilke clasped their hands in anticipation of making something which would be so beautiful. The bride's covering veil was sheer white. I wondered where the material had come from and how expensive it was, but it was something Boaz wanted me to have so I could not do anything but accept it.

The measurements were done, and fabrics chosen for my wedding robe and all days of celebration. I thought we would be ready to go home, but Naomi wanted to go to the marketplace and buy some vegetables and other foods. We did not have to be concerned about the food for the celebration as we still had not set a day when it would occur, but I overheard Naomi asking the root vegetable woman about arrangements for a large order she would place soon. I should have been more excited about my upcoming wedding, and wondered at my lack of it.

It was then I realized I missed Orpah, my family in Moab, and the life I had left behind to come with Naomi. Naomi realized I was not as joyful at having my wedding garments made as I should have been. She said, "Are you tired, Ruth?" She was selecting vegetables and fruit, turning them to see if there were any bad spots on them. Satisfied, she put them in her basket to take to the seller to purchase. "Do you want to go home?"

"I am a little tired, but we do not have to rush home," I said. Then I heard a familiar voice behind me.

"Ruth," said Miriam, "It is so wonderful to see you somewhere besides our endless days gleaning barley."

"I am so happy to see you," I said. We kissed cheeks,

smiling. "I want you to meet Naomi, my mother-in-law with whom I live. We have come from the garment makers who will sew my wedding dress and veil."

"Happy to meet you, Naomi, as Ruth has told me much about you."

"I am happy to meet you, Miriam, and glad Ruth had a friend in the field as she gleaned."

Naomi was interrupted by the root vegetable seller, who had found the leeks she was searching for.

Miriam grabbed my hand and said, "I will come around and see you soon. I am so very happy for you. Now I must be off to make supper for my husband and sons."

Naomi kept shopping, talking with shopkeepers and enjoying herself. Soon we were heading home for the day. I swept the front of our house clean of sand, and I went to fetch water from the public well. I lifted the ceramic vessel from my shoulder and filled a basin where we washed ourselves and filled one for cleaning dishes. Our routines were well set. I cut up vegetables and she did the cooking. I set out bowls for our stew. I wondered how it would be when we were in the home of Boaz and he had kitchen staff to manage almost everything. I smiled, thinking of how she had become happier here in Bethlehem. In spite of my loneliness, I was glad I had come with her. When I thought about Boaz, it brought more than a smile of joy to my face.

"Will Boaz come to sup with us tonight?" I asked, hoping for a positive answer from Naomi.

"I have not spoken with him, Ruth. You and I have been away all day deciding on your wedding garments and shopping in the marketplace." She tasted the stew she was making.

"I was only apart from you while I went for water, so neither of us have seen him. I suppose he is still busy finalizing any business he had with the harvest," I said. There was still sunlight coming in the windows, so I took up some mending and sat there to keep my mind and hands busy. I could not remember being as involved when I was anticipating my wedding with Mahlon, but then, I had been young and while Orpah and I joyously awaited our day, I was not sure then I was truly ready. Our parents handled everything. I knew I had liked Mahlon, but my inner yearnings were not nearly as strong as now when I anticipated spending my life with Boaz.

"You are too quiet, Ruth," Naomi said. She stirred stew boiling in the pot on the hearth.

"The stew smells delicious. Is it fish, vegetables, or something else you found at the market?"

"Fish and vegetables tonight. But after your fitting today, you must be thinking of your upcoming wedding, not tonight's meal."

"I was not thinking so much about the ceremony, but how different this wedding will be for me since I have been married before."

"What will be different? You and Mahlon were happy together. You will once more have a husband to provide for you and will be content with Boaz as well."

I did not want to upset her in any way, so was measuring my words carefully before I spoke. Would she think I never truly loved Mahlon? Eventually, I had loved him, but it had taken time for me to come to more than our casual friendship as young people who met and teased one another among his family's herd of sheep. I pretended to be concentrating on the seam I was mending.

"There are many more plans to make," Naomi said. When I did not comment, she said, "Our sup will be ready soon, and the sunlight is beginning to leave us. You would do well to finish the seam and wash your hands."

Would Naomi always tell me what to do as if I were a child who could not think for myself? I had come with her to take care of her and not the opposite. The meeting with Boaz and proposal I had made on the threshing floor was her plan, not mine. Now I was happy I would have a husband and a man who would look after both Naomi and me. So why should I have misgivings?

We were sitting on our mats next to the low table with our fish stew steaming in our crockery bowls in front of us. Naomi lifted her arms up in thanksgiving to Yahweh for all he had done for us. I had only dipped my spoon into the bowl when a knock upon our door startled me.

When I opened the door, it was Boaz. He was out

of breath from hurrying. "How are you and Naomi this evening? I have been meaning to come by, but have been very busy." Naomi also got up.

It was then I saw behind him a woman who was older than me. She wore a soiled robe from travel and appeared agitated, tired, or even angry.

"We are well. Please come in and bring your companion," Naomi said, ever the kind hostess to strangers. "Ruth, scoop two more bowls of stew for them."

I stepped aside, waiting for Boaz to either come in at Naomi's invitation or to decline. When he stood with a look of indecision on his face, I went to the kettle to fill two bowls with stew.

"I had not intended to stay, nor to bring this woman, but your meal smells so delicious and I am very hungry as I have been too busy to eat today."

The woman was quiet as they settled at our table. "All praise to Yahweh for providing," Boaz said, and then dipped his spoon hungrily, and tore a chunk of bread from the round in front of him.

"Are you going to tell us who your companion is?" Naomi asked.

"Gazlen is her name. She is the mother of the boy who brought my cart back to me."

Gazlen only nodded and kept slurping spoons of stew as if she had not eaten anything for a while. "Thank you for the stew and bread," Gazlen said. "I have walked a long way."

Naomi and I were awaiting some explanation for

the appearance of the woman, but neither of them said anything about it. Naomi finally asked, "Did you come from town by the Synagogue? It is a long way."

Boaz nodded. Gazlen did not answer Naomi. I thought about what I had heard about the mother of Silas beating him for little or no offense, and the sad condition of his clothing and seemingly starved body. I wondered if this was the boy's mother come to get him home or to beg for money. If all of what I had heard was true, I hoped Boaz would find work for the boy, take care of him, and send his mother back home without him.

Gazlen had cleaned her bowl, sopped the last with bread, and looked up. "Would you like more?" I asked. She only nodded.

I scooped another bowl of stew for her, and she started eating hungrily, making loud slurping noises, as if she had not already eaten a bowl full.

Boaz looked from Naomi to me and back at Gazlen. "I suppose I need to explain who this woman is, and what she is doing in Bethlehem."

Gazlen stood up. Her bowl was empty, and I thought she meant to leave. Instead, she said, "Boaz has enticed my son Silas to come here. I am trying to get him to release the boy back into my care as I need him to help me. Now you have filled your belly, Boaz, please show me where you have hidden my son or I will call the authorities." Her voice was bold and hard.

Boaz stood, shook his head in disgust, and said,

"Have a good evening my dear friends, and thank you for the wonderful stew and bread." He kissed Naomi's cheeks and then mine, then followed the woman out the door.

Naomi and I stood gaping at each other at the strange turn of events this evening. "He did not expect I would invite them both to sup. She looked like a terrible person."

"I wonder what will happen," I moaned. I put my face in my hands and began to cry. All of the events leading up to the boy coming and his mother following him began when he agreed on the threshing room floor to be the kinsman redeemer. His way of handling everything according to the tradition of the law and Synagogue records, sent him off to the Synagogue to make sure his acquiring of Elimelech's property including me was recorded legally.

Naomi said, "Do not fear, Boaz will know how to handle the situation with the boy and his mother."

I nodded to her, but kept remembering my shock at seeing such a woman darken our door, and I remained unsettled.

17. Boaz

A cheerful heart is good medicine,
but a downcast spirit dries up the bones.

Proverbs 17: 22

As I walked toward my property with Gazlen, I wondered what else could happen, and how I would handle the trouble I now faced because of her coming for her son. When I had gone out to the tethered nag earlier, thinking the horse was the reason for the outbreak of unrest, I saw Gazlen screaming something I couldn't understand at my workers there by the animal pens. She then had followed me all the way to the threshing barn and created havoc there demanding I produce the boy. I asked her to be patient as I had work to be done. She was not easily put off.

I stopped to visit Naomi and Ruth to see how they were doing, and Naomi asked Gazlen and me to come in. Since I was hungry and wanted to see Ruth, I went in. I was thankful Gazlen did not make too much fuss there. I believe food kept her calm.

Unsure what to do next, I came home, but did not invite the woman in. She refused to wait at first, when I asked her to. When she kept up her demands, I said I needed to find out if anyone inside knew anything about the boy's whereabouts. Cook was going about his cooking, but Sarai was not in the kitchen, and thankfully, neither was Silas. "Where is Sarai?" I asked.

"At home, but will be here soon. She heard from your animal workers the boy's mother had shown up and had demanded he be returned. Sarai's keeping him quiet at home. I waited until you returned to find out what you wanted to do about Silas. He is so young and has reported poor treatment by his mother, which one can see from his appearance. Do you think she would let him stay if she knew he had us to care for him? The boy said his mother depends on money from his begging, and he indicated she has many men who visit with her and do something while he has to remain away. Afterwards, she always has some money, but is unhappy." Cook looked knowingly at me, and I understood the woman was a prostitute.

"If you and Sarai would like to have him as a kitchen helper, I see no reason for him to go back with his mother except her selfishness and greed. I do not know how I can convince her to leave without him, unless I lie and say he has gone. I do not think she would like to have the income she got from his begging suddenly disappear. Whether she would go to the authorities as she has threatened, or would leave peaceably I cannot know."

The woman was still out front when I came back. "He is not in my kitchen or my house. He was here eating earlier in the day."

"Where do you suppose he has gone?" Her arms were folded across her chest and her chin jutted out. "Where? Where is my son?" She raised her voice and had her mouth open as if to scream again when we both saw Silas walking up casually.

"I am here, Mother," Silas answered. "I returned the cart and donkey as you asked me to do, and these nice people have fed me, given me a soft mat on which to sleep. Please do not trouble Boaz or his people, for he has been good to me. I want to stay here." He wore clean clothing, and his voice was clear as he was rested and fed.

Gazlen had expected a fight, but there was none, except her son wanted to stay with me, not her. She relaxed her arms and started to laugh. "How long do you think they will put up with your laziness? And your lies? He does not know you as I do. I did not ask you to return the man's donkey and cart. It was a lie you told."

I watched Silas's reaction to his mother. I had fully intended to keep him hidden, and create a ruse saying he had left, but the boy had decided to handle things in his own way. While I marveled at his bravery, I felt fairly sure she would not hear of him staying with me. He was too valuable to her as a beggar. Now he would have to go back to a miserable life.

Cook came out with Sarai. "I am Cook and this is my wife Sarai. The boy stayed at our humble home last night. My wife, whom you can see has a lame leg as she walks, cannot do all the sweeping and household chores. I have to be at work in the kitchen here. We were wondering if you would allow Silas to live with us and do work for us at least for a time to see how it goes. He could go home any time he chooses, so he would not be a slave. What do you say?" Cook wore common plain clothing, so she could see he was not a land owner or businessman.

Gazlen looked from one to the other of us, shaking her head. By the look on her face, perhaps she felt outnumbered, at least something had perplexed her.

Silas went to his mother and stood by her side, then asked, "May I try to do this? I want to help the good woman who is lame. If it does not work out, I will return to you." He reached for her hand, but she withdrew it.

"They will make a slave of you, and will not let you ever return to me. I do not trust them, as look at this fine home and property. Did Boaz get this honestly? They do not need a boy, as the man here can hire anyone they choose. If you manage to escape, I will be waiting for you. Meanwhile, Boaz and I have some business we need to discuss."

"I have work to do in the kitchen," Cook said. Sarai followed him and motioned for Silas to come. The boy hesitated, but I nodded to him and he followed them inside.

Gazlen held her hand out, "You owe me for the boy," she said. While I did not want my kindness for the boy to be anything else, I knew the only way Gazlen would leave is if I crossed her palm with money. I gave her more than she asked, and bid her to leave. "If you wish, you may take the donkey and cart, or the old nag tethered over there," I said. "But you must leave and do not come back here again. Silas can leave any time he wants." She shook her head and turned away from me. I watched as she hoisted herself up on the old nag with the help of a rope and led the horse out of the pen. She must have ridden a horse before.

+++

The next day, Cook and Sarai were in the kitchen making our breakfast. Silas was washing cooking vessels. It looked like a good work crew and made me smile. I started to talk with them about the upcoming wedding celebration plans and foods I would want the kitchen to prepare. It would require more than the three of them. After our conversation, I went to my animal workers and inquired as to any fatted calves and lambs. I was presented with three calves and three lambs for my inspection. We also had a fowler who would bring down game hens to roast. In Bethlehem, there was a fisher who often brought in catch. Later, I went to see Naomi and Ruth to discuss the meal plans for the celebration, which would last six days, excluding the Sabbath.

"Boaz, how nice to see you," Ruth said, as she answered my knock on the door. She looked behind me, lest I had Gazlen with me as I had on my last visit.

"It is wonderful to see you, dear Ruth, and no, I have no one with me. In fact, the boy's mother has gone back home, but without her son. I will explain later."

"I trust you are here to discuss a wedding," Naomi said, as I came inside with Ruth.

"I now have a day scheduled for the big event," I said. "Will one month be enough time to get it all together? I saw the clothier for my robe and Shnayder said you had been in for fittings and garment decisions.

I have the fatted calves and lambs we will need, but you will need to procure the fish from James so he will save the catch for us then. You will ask the people in the marketplace to have ready many vegetables, fruits, and perhaps honey cakes. I will ask Cook to make sure there are sufficient ingredients for the bread which they will need to bake for the wedding feast. I have someone in mind to create for me another large oven for baking enough bread."

Ruth and Naomi both looked on with smiles on their faces. "Rabbi Matteaus will have to be contacted now the actual time had been set for our wedding. I will see to it soon." I was still standing and talking, with all these things on my mind when Naomi said, "Boaz, won't you sit?" I sat on a tan cushion by the low table. She brought out wine and bread, and we three sat, continuing to make plans.

"Will you call on our neighbors and friends in Bethlehen to invite them? How many people will we need to prepare food for? And musicians?" Naomi had a keen mind and was not missing anything.

"We must have dancing! I do not know musicians who would play for our dancing, Weddings did not occur during the drought years, and I have not attended any in recent time. There must be musicians who play flutes, tambourines, horns, drums or anything around here. Our celebration plans should not be without music and dancing."

Suddenly Naomi looked distressed, and I was not

sure why. Ruth looked away. I wondered what had gotten into these two. Maybe we were trying to discuss too much all at once. It was as if the whole conversation came to a halt when I had talked about music and dancing. It should have been a joyful topic, not the opposite. I finished my wine and rose to go as I realized I must have brought up a sore subject, although I did not know why it would be. "I need to visit Rabbi Matteaus and let him know when he will preside over our sacred rites," I said, trying to sound bright and cheerful despite the obvious dull atmosphere. I cheek-kissed them both and left.

Some workers were still busy in my threshing barn as I went to see how things were progressing. Except for some foolish comments about Gazlen having some business with me, not much was said as they were interested in finishing and going on to another field. I waved them off, laughing at the absurdity. "I am marrying soon!" While most of my field servants would not have an invitation, everyone would be talking about the wedding.

I went to see Rabbi Matteaus. He did have the date open I had selected for the celebration of our wedding. We did not have to discuss any particulars, as nuptials and weddings were always done in the same way. He asked, "Have you gotten a carpenter to erect a canopy for the day you and Ruth will say your vows?"

His easy demeanor gave me the reassurance he knew everything I would need to do.

"Do you have a man you would recommend who could build it?" We were sitting in the shade of an old olive tree in front of his house.

"Yes, my cousin Shad has a carpentry trade and has built many before. It is a simple structure and can be taken down easily. He will be able to do it quickly. You may know him."

I knew Shad as he had built the extra rooms in my house before Ruth and Naomi would come to live with me. He was delighted to get the job and wished me well. Everything seemed to be going smoothly so far as our plans were concerned. I still did not know what had caused Naomi and then Ruth to become almost sad at my mention of dancing. Perhaps next, I should speak with Ruth privately.

Ruth was on her way out the door with a jar to go fetch water when I arrived. "Ruth, why don't I come along and discuss with you what I have done this morning?" I took the big jug and kissed both her cheeks. I told her how things had gone with Silas, and his mother had gone back home.

"I am happy for Silas, so he will be helping Cook and Sarai now."

"Yes, and today I saw Rabbi Matteaus, who has agreed to be there to read our sacred rites. And Shad will construct our canopy. It will need some decorating, which I will try to get some of my servant women to do."

Ruth clapped her hands joyfully, and I was glad to

see she was not still downcast as she had been when I last saw her. "I can almost not believe my good fortune," she said.

"It is good to see your happy anticipation. I was not so sure when I last saw you and Naomi and you both had saddened faces when I talked about dancing at our wedding. Was something wrong with what I said?"

Ruth did not answer at first. The day was warm with a gentle breeze which cooled us nicely. We had gotten to the well, and I dipped the bucket to fill her water jar. Finally, she cleared her throat and said, "Elimelech fell ill during the middle of a dance at Mahlon's and my wedding. He never truly recovered and then died. Naomi was saddened to remember it, and I could sense her grief. I am sorry we did not express ourselves when you talked so happily about music and dancing. It should have been at least as exciting as all the food." Ruth's smile was captivating.

"I am glad you told me the reason. It is understandable Naomi would recall what happened and be sad. We will both be careful how we approach the subject of music again. Perhaps I will not mention dancing." I looked at Ruth tenderly. She would be a wonderful partner to me. After I filled the stone jar, I carried it home for her.

18. Ruth

A word fitly spoken is like apples of gold in a setting of silver.

Proverbs 25: 11

Boaz kissed my cheeks as we got back to Naomi's house. I went in with the water and put fresh water in our basin for washing. I hummed while I worked and Naomi smiled at my joy. "You are especially happy; did you see Boaz on your way?"

"Yes, he has been to Rabbi Matteaus and has everything arranged with him. He has Shad building our canopy."

"I heard from neighbors how Silas is staying on with Boaz, and his mother rode the old nag back to her home. News travels about, doesn't it?"

"All true. Are we to go back to the clothier to see how they are doing with the wedding garments?"

"Yes, tomorrow we will go see. Rebekah is working with them in the shop now. I will also ask them to create a new robe for me to wear." Naomi was smiling, the sadness of the thought of music and wedding dancing behind her for now.

+++

We came into Shnayder's clothes shop. They were busy as were the women who sew for them. Rebekah nodded to us as she was busy sewing. Shpilke greeted us warmly. "I have something beautiful for you to see and try on!" She said.

She took some robes from where they hung for me to inspect. All three of them were lovely and fit for a queen. I slipped each one on and every item was met with appreciative sounds from the women who were sewing. Naomi smiled and said, "You look so beautiful. I love the way the colors look with your skin and hair. We must find some jewels fitting for them."

I wished for a quiet pool of water where I could see my reflection, but took their admiration for my answer as to how I looked when I tried it on. "Thank you, I can hardly wait until you complete the dress for my wedding day."

Shpilke handed me some under garments which would be worn beneath the robes. If it was warm for our wedding celebration, the soft cottons would absorb the wetness of my skin. "We are still doing the sewing and embroidered designs needed for your wedding robe," she said.

Naomi selected some fabric and asked them to create a new robe for her to wear. Rebekah volunteered to sew Naomi's robe. I looked on with interest, as there would be more than one day to wear her fine new robe. "Will you need only one?" I asked.

"I have other wearables, so one will do," she said. "I am not the one who must dress to shine for others to admire."

"Mother, you are doing so much planning for my wedding, and I think you will want at least another new garment." I looked earnestly at her, as I thought of her as my mother. I wanted the best for her too.

Shpilke nodded, and brought out another fabric, one carefully dyed with yellow, red, and rare blue. It was one I had missed when I had looked. Naomi drew in her breath in admiration. "Yes, I like it, but will it cost a lot of money?"

"We are creating all of the wedding garments and Boaz has told us he is paying for everything. Naomi, we are making your personal robes for the cost of the fabric and nothing more," Shpilke said.

Once we were at home I wondered if Boaz had done anything about musicians, but thought it best not to bring it up with Naomi. If I were to see him again alone, I would inquire. Despite Naomi's bad memories of dancing and then losing Elimelech, we would surely want music and at least a traditional, joyful hora. I was awhirl with many thoughts. Suddenly it was as if a wound existed deep inside of me. I could not think of anything except Mahlon, and a feeling of guilt at finding love again.

What of Orpah; was she married again? I had heard no news from Moab at all, and would not bring up the subject of trying to send a runner to Moab to invite my parents and brother Ammon who would probably be married by now. Perhaps it was because I was making wedding plans, but I sorely missed Orpah. We had been such close friends, and shared in joy and sorrow together.

Naomi was busy in the kitchen as usual, but left it, and came to sit with me on our beige cushions where I was simply gazing off at nothing in particular. "Ruth, would you like for us to get a runner to go to Moab and see if your family would like to come attend the wedding. I know you are missing your friend Orpah. I miss the girl too."

Surprised, I turned to her smiling, my melancholy stilled. "Is there any way we could arrange to have a runner go all the way to Moab? I wonder if there would be time for someone to go and my family to come before our wedding next month, even if a runner left now on a fast steed."

"You may be right, but even if they could not come, perhaps we could send word so your parents, brother, and Orpah would all know you are doing well."

The thought of it uplifted my mood and I was happier. "Thank you, Naomi," I said. I reached over and hugged her shoulders.

When Boaz came the next day, Naomi discussed sending a runner to Moab with him. "I know a man I can send," Boaz said. "He works with my animals and his brother has a good fast horse he may ride. I can spare him for a week or so. There may not be time for your parents to come, but at least they will know about your wedding."

He did not stay to sup, but we kissed cheeks and he left to take care of all he had to accomplish.

The next day we went to the clothier to see my garment I would wear for the wedding day rites. Shpilke had it draped across a large cushion. There it was, and it was so very lovely I could not picture myself in anything so fine. The red silken sash was loose and ready to be tied around my ivory white robe. The floral white embroidery on the white robe was done in some shiny imported threads which were shimmering in the bright sunlight shining in the window. When I tried it on it fit and was not too long or too short. Shpilke, Shnayder, Rebekah and the sewing women all smiled at my appearance when I tried it on. One of Naomi's robes was finished and the other was promised in a few days.

After the excitement of our clothing being ready, there was not much for Naomi and me to do toward the wedding. Everything else was arranged and in place to be done for the celebration and feast to come.

It seemed the day would take forever to come, and yet it did. Naomi and I moved to rooms in the house of Boaz and closed the house in town. Neighbors all wished us well, and many would be at our wedding. We readied ourselves, dressing for the first day of the week-long celebration. I wore my yellow robe for the first day as we greeted people coming from afar. Since I had heard nothing from the runner, and truly did not know if such a thing had even happened, I did not expect I would hear anything from my family or Orpah. Boaz and I were not to be together before the ceremony at all. We could see each other in a group of guests, but could not go off and talk alone. I saw Cook and Sarai supervising the loading of food carts to bring to the tables. Cook also was the wine steward, and saw to the tasting and pouring for the guests. They were jovial and happy. I wanted to ask if Silas was still there with them as I had not seen him. Perhaps the boy had become lonesome for his mother and returned to her.

On the second day of celebration, more people arrived, some with a distance to travel had tents in which to stay. It looked so festive, and seemed much larger than my first wedding. Silas was working with Cook and Sarai was doing something inside in the kitchen so she did not have to be using her lame leg so much. The boy smiled happily as he worked, and I saw fine hair beginning to sprout on his chin. He had good skin color now, not so sallow, and had gained some body strength since he had been under their care.

On the third day, my spirits soared with joy. Musicians had arrived from somewhere and were playing tambourines, drums, flutes, and horns, which created a happy background for all the crowd gathered there. And the next day was much the same. I had not seen Boaz, but at a distance all these days. I wore another new robe, which was of many colors. Many people complimented my appearance.

It was the day before our ceremony. I awakened early and heard a commotion outside somewhere. I wondered if guests had already become drunken so early in the day. Naomi came to my door. "Someone has an important message for you, Ruth."

19. Boaz

For everything there is a season,
and a time for every matter under heaven.

Ecclesiastes 3: 1

The couple arrived in the midst of the weeklong celebration of our wedding. I saw Ruth across the expanse of guests now and then, but never up close. A small entourage of servants came with the couple as they rode up in a serviceable travel cart drawn by two donkeys. Excitement filled the air as I was told to greet them and welcome them as they had traveled hastily from Moab. I had never met any of Ruth's family, nor any from Moab. "Who has come?" I asked someone.

"See for yourself. It is a fine-looking couple."

I went to the cart to welcome them as they had already alit. "Welcome to the wedding celebration. I am the host, Boaz."

"I am Ammon, Ruth's brother."

I grasped his shoulders, smiling. "I am truly happy you could come as I sent a runner to let her family know she was marrying me. And you have your wife with you." She stepped to his side, and waited.

I called to one of my servants, "Please tell Ruth her brother has a message for her."

Ammon grinned mischievously to me. "We will see if my sister is curious to know what the message might be. I can hardly wait to see her face when she sees I have come to deliver my message personally."

Ruth came out after no one would give her the message and insisted she come to hear it instead.

Ruth and Naomi both came. I stepped away so as not to break the vow of keeping a distance before the ceremony. I could still see and hear everything.

"Ammon!" Ruth squealed, and turned to the woman beside him. "Orpah! You both came." They all embraced and sobbed happy tears. Ammon stepped back and put one arm around Orpah's shoulder."

"I would like to present to you my wife, your friend, Orpah."

Ruth dissolved into more tears as she and Orpah hugged again. Naomi and Orpah embraced warmly as well, and Ammon kissed Naomi's cheeks. I thought I had never seen such a happy reunion.

Good news is sometimes accompanied by other information which is not so welcome to hear. Ruth's father died shortly after Ammon and Orpah married, but it did not seem to dampen her spirits. Her mother, grown frail, had declined to come. Ruth's elation at knowing her best friend had married her brother, and they had both rushed a distance to get to her wedding made any other news pale in comparison. They could stay for the rest of our celebration and another day to rest before they needed to head back as Ammon had his father's property to take care of as well as his own.

I asked Silas to see to their donkeys needs for water and food, and a shady place to bed down near my animals. Another two servants were to see to the unloading of their things from the cart and show them to rooms in my home.

+++

The day had come we would say our sacred vows

before Yahweh, words Rabbi Matteaus would have us say, and would be witnessed by our family and friends who were present. I washed, trimmed my beard, and dressed carefully in my new robe of fine cotton which had been expertly sewn by the clothier Shnayder and his sewing women. I had a shiny metal knife in my room with a broad blade in which I could see my face after the trim. My man-servant came and approved of my appearance. "You may go, Elkan, I believe we have done all we could with this old body," I said to him.

"You look well for an old man." Elkan nodded, chuckled, and had a pleasant look on his face as he left the room. I smiled at his teasing. He and I had known each other since were both young boys. His father had lost everything during our dry years and had died from unknown causes. I had asked him to come throughout the rest of the drought in my home so he would not be alone. He had not married. I had not asked Elkan to work for me, but he had insisted once I became very busy after the drought came to an end.

Music was not playing today until after our ceremony. The canopy was a thing of beauty. Shpilke had brought fabrics, and my servant women had made cloth streamers of white and green to decorate it. A white cloth was draped across the top and back to create a shade for us. White symbolized purity, and green symbolized new life. My pulse beat strongly with the excitement. A day I had once thought had passed me by due to circumstances was about to occur. My father had once wisely said, "To everything there is a season, and a time for every purpose under heaven." While it had been many years since he was alive, I still remembered many of his teachings.

I came out of my house at the appropriate time and Rabbi Matteaus met me to escort me to our canopy. We waited there as the sun beat down around us all. It was late in the day as was customary, so when the stars appeared in heaven they would shine down upon us and remind us of the myriad miracles and children Yahweh would bring to a married couple.

And then I beheld Ruth, dressed in white with a red sash, with a white drape covering her lovely face. I knew how beautiful her face appeared beneath her thin cloth veil. She walked slowly forward until she was beneath the canopy with the Rabbi and me. I read the words of promise:

I, Boaz, promise to: feed my wife; clothe her; and provide her conjugal needs. My estate is obligated to pay her a lump sum in the event that I divorce her or die before she did. I must and will pay her medical bills if she falls ill; and ransom her if she is taken hostage. If my wife passes away before me, I must pay her burial expenses, and after I die, her children inherit their mother's ketubah money before the rest of the estate is divided amongst all the heirs. In the event that I, her husband, die before my wife, Ruth, she is entitled to live in my home and live off my estate until she dies or remarries, and her daughters, too, are to be supported by the estate until they marry.

Ruth promised to respect me and live with me, so we might bear children together.

It was a very exciting moment for me as I had thought a day such as this would never come for me. The air was warm, but not overly so. The evening stars were beginning to appear in the heavens as the sun settled below the rim of the earth. A light breeze ruffled the streamers and covering of the canopy. The crowd of guests could be heard whispering or murmuring, but everything was mostly quiet and calm. I drank it all in as if sipping a fine wine. And I could not wait to see Ruth until the time came for me to lift her veil and behold her beautiful, radiant face. She seemed especially happy. Her smile would have charmed the angels.

It was not traditional for us to embrace or kiss in front of everyone. Rabbi Matteaus presented us as married to all those in attendance. With our hands clasped, we walked side by side toward my home and into its open door as was appropriate and expected.

20. Ruth

Boaz took Ruth and she became his wife.

Ruth 4: 13a

My wedding celebration took on a whole new joy, as Orpah and my brother Ammon came from my home town and told me they were married. While Moab, and my young life there were well in my past, I still had longed to see my friend Orpah, who had been my closest companion all the years I could remember. Since she married my brother Ammon, I was even more elated to see them.

The streamers on the canopy waved in the breeze as I beheld it from a window in the room I shared with Naomi. Orpah begged to come and help me. Mostly, she wanted to spend as much time visiting with me as she could before I would be too occupied to give her any time. We reminisced about old times together as we lay on a mat and giggled like girls. We talked until it was time for me to dress. Naomi wanted to do the motherly help with my sash and my hair.

Orpah suggested braiding and wrapping the braid up high like a crown, letting the rest of my shining hair flow down in a cascade. Naomi wove a white ribbon into the braid and let the ends stream down my back with my dark brown hair. They both approved of my appearance. I was excited, but anxious, not knowing what to expect from Boaz as he was a little older and wiser and more experienced than Mahlon had been. I kept the thoughts to myself. I wanted the best to come from this marriage, especially for Naomi. One nagging thought kept coming back to me: I had never had a child when I was married to Mahlon. I was barren, or presumably so. Should I tell Boaz? Or would he realize since I had no children it must mean I was barren.

When we had said our vows, and walked into Boaz' house to consummate our marriage, I kept worrying about how to tell him my concern.

At first, he planted holy kisses on my cheeks, then sought my lips. He crushed me in his arms and his lips and mouth kept insistently pressing on mine.

"I hope I have not bruised your tender lips," he said, drawing back slightly.

"My I undress you?" He was almost breathless.

"Yes, as you wish." I nodded.

He treated me like a precious gift, and wanted to undress me as one would open a parcel of surprises. I hoped he would not be disappointed. His eyes feasted on me in my robe at first, then slowly untied my sash, and unwrapped my robe. "Ruth, my wife, I can hardly believe you are really here with me. You are mine."

Boaz removed my sash, and placed it carefully on a plush green cushion. Then he unwrapped my beautiful white silken floral embroidered robe to reveal the plain cotton tunic which fit me loosely. He slipped it off easily. He gazed in awe and said, "It is as if I have unwrapped the most precious gift I am about to hold in my arms and have to hold forever in my life. Only in my dreams have I even imagined what it would be like to behold such a very beautiful woman as you."

It was as if a divine presence enveloped us and I saw Boaz sensed it as well. It seemed as if we were part of a history yet unwritten, but we did not know what it was. The delicious feeling stayed with me on into the night when we were naked in bed together. I paid no mind to the celebrants milling around outside, the men making merry and talking, and the women at the food tables. Servants were busy setting out all the food for the feast. Music played.

Perhaps my timing was off, and I did not want to break the deliciousness of this moment, but I was impelled to tell Boaz. I needed to get it out of the way, so I told him, "I am barren, as I had no children with Mahlon."

"Perhaps Yahweh was not ready to open your womb then. You were very young. He brought you here to me for a reason. Let us not spoil the moment doubting what he can do for you and me." He held me in a deep embrace, kissed me passionately on the mouth as never before, and I could feel his male member grown hard against my thigh.

"My love for you has deepened," I whispered.

I admired his muscled arms, his capable hands, large enough, yet soft as they caressed my body when we lay together. I opened his shirt and saw the well-formed chest with a small forest of black hair. I did not know if he expected me to admire him with words as he had me, so I only gestured my appreciation by placing my hands on his chest, caressing him. As I did so, I sighed involuntarily. I closed my eyes as joy-filled tears wanted to spill out.

Since I had been a wife a while ago, I knew how it would be with us as a couple to become one. It had been a little different as to our celebration here than the first time, as Mahlon and I had joined in the dancing before consummating our marriage. The men had lifted him and his brother high in the air, teasing them, and rambunctiously kicked up their legs in dance. We women had gathered in a hora circle and danced. Much time was spent dancing before we actually went in to complete our marriage in bed together. This entire week, the dancing had taken place before the rites had been performed under our canopy today. Once we were joined as one, we would spend the rest of our night together while the guests danced and ate and visited before finally retiring to their own beds.

I had a floating sensation as our coupling filled my breasts, my thighs, my belly with ecstatic joy with all the caresses Boaz gave me. Had I ever been so loved? I could not remember, nor did I want to. When we were both very wet in all our bodily places, he came in to my body and we were whole. I lay still and contented.

"I will love you forever, Ruth," Boaz said. He was on his side, his elbow supported him so he could look at me with those dreamy dark gold-flecked eyes.

My eyes beheld his wonderful body, strong from hard work as we lay there drinking in each other in the after-glow of our lovemaking. Telling him I loved him did not seem enough at this moment in time. I reached out and stroked his leg. "You are even more than life to me. My love for you has deepened since we have become one. I cannot explain it, yet it is real. I love you."

We heard the murmur of the guests below once the music had stopped for the evening. Some were already gone to their homes or wherever they had decided to go for the night. We would have one more day of feast and celebration tomorrow until sundown. Sabbath would be then, when no work or celebration would take place.

We fell asleep naked in each other's arms. In the morning, the sun streamed in our window and I forgot for a moment where I was. Boaz was no longer abed. He must have gone down to see to the day's activities as people would be eating breakfast here, visiting, and soon music and dancing would begin. A servant girl knocked on the door and I bid her to enter. "Come in. What is your name?"

"I am Marta, here to help you dress and to clean your room."

"Thank you, I must relieve myself and then wash first." I unwrapped the light cover and I stood, trying not to be too ashamed at my nakedness.

She did not look at me. She produced a chamber pot which had been in the corner of the room. And a small table held a basin of water, some nice smelling herbal soap liquid, and next to it was a cloth towel with which to dry myself. After I had taken care of my personal cleanliness, I saw she had already hung my wedding garment and folded my under-tunic.

"Naomi gave me this robe for you to wear today," she said. In her hand was a robe I had not requested to be made for myself. It was a beautiful cotton of yellow, creamy white, and green, with a small stripe of blue around the hem. I presumed it was a gift from Naomi. Marta helped me put it on, admiring the way it looked on me. I was hungry and thirsty, but did not know if I should go down yet.

Orpah knocked on my door, "Get up, Ruth, I do not have much more time to visit with you before Ammon and I have to make our trek back to Moab."

"I am up," I declared, as I met her at the door, "And I am thirsty and hungry."

We hurried down together and met Ammon, who was already eating bread and sipping a morning cup of tea. We soon joined him at a low table where women put more food in front of us than we could possibly eat, and Cook came to bring some fresh breakfast wine, which was not fermented, but sweet red grape juice. Years we had been apart evaporated as Orpah and I talked like we always had as youngsters. Orpah stopped eating the fig she had started to bite into. "Traveling has given my stomach some ills," she said.

I remembered when she had been ill when she was expecting Hester, but I could not bring myself to think about what her problem might now be. I wondered if she would soon discover she was "with child," and for both her and my brother I hoped it was so. I vowed to myself not to be envious, but joyful for them.

Boaz joined us, laughing. "It did not take you long to get together this morning, I see. I went to my chamber and the servant told me you had gone out with your friend."

Everyone was soon eating, visiting and once the music began, some people were dancing. Boaz and I joined hands and he swept me out to join the group dancing in a large circle with women on the outside and men inside, each one trying, but not succeeding in getting a woman to dance only with him. Many groped at me, trying to annoy Boaz. Laughter and good-natured teasing kept up until the musicians took a break.

At our final celebration meal, Boaz raised his wine goblet wishing to all health, and joy and, "Shalom, shalom!"

I hugged Orpah and Ammon, as did Naomi. Boaz embraced both Ammon and Orpah together within his expansive arms as we all bid them a safe journey back to Moab. "Thank you for coming to our wedding. I appreciate the effort it must have taken to make such a trip on a short notice. You may stay as long as you wish, and please come visit again," Boaz said.

"We were happy to be invited to your wedding, and thank your Cook and Sarai for preparing a lot of food for us for our journey home." Ammon said. Both expressed their appreciation of his hospitality, and Ammon went to make sure his donkeys and cart were all hitched and ready for their long trek.

Orpah and I shared one last hug, and she said quietly, "Ammon and I may be expecting a child; and I hope I will not be too ill on our way back home. I pray your God will bless you and Boaz."

"All is ready, and we must be off if we want to be in a good place to settle when daylight has ended. Come, Orpah." He held out his hand to Orpah, and I could see he loved her. The cart wheels made little dust circles in the air as they rolled away. I was sad to see them go, but I knew my brother had to go back to care for all the lands where he now grew spelt and barley and raised cattle and sheep.

Sadness crept up on me, and I turned away from watching them leave. I realized I might never see them again, and a part of my life had left with them along with the happy memories. While I was hopeful for my future with Boaz and was reassured Naomi and I would be cared for, I could not entirely shake off the melancholy. Then, among the guests I saw my friend Miriam. She smiled and came to me to congratulate me. "I met your friend Orpah and your brother," she said.

"I'm so glad you met as you are both my friends."

+++

I was lost in my own thoughts as I came to the kitchen next morning, which was the Sabbath. Bread and fresh grape juice were on the table for me to eat. No one was cooking out of respect for the Sabbath law of no work. Sarai was sitting there. "God's good day, Sarai, you should be home abed with Cook after so many days of cooking for all our guests."

"He is not happy today, as Silas has taken missing. We do not know when he left, or what has happened to him. Perhaps he went home to his mother."

21. Boaz

Just as water reflects the face,
So, one human heart reflects another.

Proverbs 27: 19

Our celebration was over. Sabbath was quiet as no work was being done. Ruth and I slept together on Sabbath night, but she seemed to be somewhere else, not wholly present with me. Did she know I could already sense her thoughts before she expressed them, or did not share them at all? Oneness with her was a new experience for me, something I had never had before. It was beautiful, powerful, and carried a big responsibility for me, her happiness. What I knew she wanted more than anything was to become a mother. Very much aware I was an older man, but still a capable one, I hoped Yahweh would open us both to the joy of having a child.

I was grateful for the Sabbath day of rest. Soon, I would be busy with dealings with the grain which we had harvested and were storing and selling. Another growing crop, one which would be cut for hay for cattle and stalls, demanded my attention.

When I came to the kitchen for my breakfast which had been placed on the table the night before, Ruth and Sarai were sitting together talking. Sarai sounded upset about something. "What troubles you?" I asked.

"Silas is gone. He had become like a son instead of a mere servant to me. I do not know why he has left, but disappeared some time during the week of celebration. I was too busy to notice at first, but Cook asked me if I knew where he was as he needed him to refill a tray of food. We thought Silas had become tired and gone off somewhere to rest, but we had no time to look for him," Sarai said.

"I do not know why he would have gone back to his mother as he has been happy here. You have given him good care, a home, food and clothing as he has not had before. I will ask around to see if anyone has seen him." I ate with them, and Ruth and I went to sit in the shade with our morning wine. She seemed to be less sad than yesterday when her brother and friend left. The gentle breeze wafted around us as we talked quietly about our lives going forward. Both of us were concerned about Silas, but sure he was able to take care of himself whatever he had decided to do. In some ways, due to his upbringing on his own in the streets he was wise beyond his years.

"I have good news," Ruth suddenly brightened, "My friend Orpah told me she is expecting a child."

"If Yahweh is willing, soon you and I may share good news such as your friend gave to you." I patted her soft hand and grasped it in mine, marveling at its smallness and softness since she had not recently been in my fields handling dry stalks and grain heads.

She said nothing, only smiled shyly at me. I vowed to do my part to make a child happen for us and for our family heritage in years to come.

Life carried on as the weeks progressed. Some days I came home worn out and in need only of rest, I thought. Ruth would meet me, and put her arms out for me to hug. I could not resist such love. She would take my hand and lead me to a bath I had men dig and create for us, and we both dipped into it after shedding our garments. We then would dress. and dine on whatever Cook had prepared for us. Some evenings I wanted more than a cup of wine to relax my bones. She often sensed it and coaxed me to bed, whether to give me a back rub, or for lovemaking.

Some mornings she was still abed when I rose to go to the barns or fields. I let her sleep as much as she chose. Naomi was content in my home. All seemed well in my household, and I was grateful my life had become so full. I was blessed to be this family's redeemer.

One day while I was busy in Bethlehem with business, I saw an unmistakable form dart behind a building. I had to find out if it was Silas, and walked quickly to the spot I had seen him run to. He was crouched behind a bush, but it did little to hide him. "Come out and explain your absence," I said.

His hair was tangled, and his clothes were soiled as he crept out on all fours, not standing, but groveling in front of me. "Master Boaz, I am once more tired and hungry. I cannot seem to make my way begging here in Bethlehem. They took one look at my nice robe and laughed at me."

"Get up, son, why did you think you needed to go away and fend for yourself? Were you not well cared for in the home of Sarai and Cook? If not, did you not remember my kindness to you? Sarai is grieved with worry about you. I ought to beat you with a stick for causing so much worry and sorrow with your actions."

"Beat me. I deserve to be punished; I am not a

good person, not like all of you. I am sorry I made the good woman sad by my running away. I am not used to anyone caring so much about me. I thought if I made enough money begging, I could grow to be a wealthy man like you and have a wife." He stood, sad-faced.

I grabbed him, lifted him off his feet and shook him like a bundle of grain, then I enfolded him in a fatherly embrace. "Do not ever run away again," I said. "Now we will go back to my home and you can face it like a man, and explain yourself to Cook and Sarai." He tried not to let me see tears streaming down his cheeks. I think he was glad I had found him, but disappointed his decision to try to support himself had not turned out well.

Cook scolded Silas, and then he and Sarai took him home to get cleaned up and ready to work in the kitchen with them again, after first asking if he was willing to come back to them under the same terms as before he had run off. He was grateful to have a home, a job to do and their care over him. "I am sorry I worried you," he said to Sarai. "I will never go off again without telling you both."

+++

Ruth had taken up a sewing task, mending some of Silas's torn garments. He sometimes climbed trees, and did all manner of things young boys do to amuse themselves which meant he snagged and tore a sleeve or other part of his garment on something. She looked so sweet to me, sitting in fading sunlight with needle and thread poised in her hand. Her face had rounded some and taken on a glow lately. I could not keep my eyes off her whether clothed or naked in my bed with me. I hoped I did not couple with her too often, but she never complained of my need for her body in our lovemaking.

One morning it all changed. She did not come to breakfast, even though I had not left early for a day in the fields. A servant later said Ruth was not well. I did not enquire further, as I knew women sometimes had reasons not to go out among people and wanted to stay to themselves. Naomi told me she would look in on her. That evening, Ruth did not greet me and was not in my room when I went up to my bed. I became worried, but decided it must be her moon cycle. A servant knocked on my door and told me Ruth was sleeping in a bed in Naomi's room for the night. Since I had never had a woman in my house, I had neglected to have a mikvah made for her cleansing after a moon cycle. I would have the same men who made my bath dig one for her, smooth the sides with cleaned flat stones and fill it with water.

Days passed without Ruth. She had closed herself away from me, and I realized it was likely the same for all married men. Soon I would see her again so we could resume our marital relations. Would Yahweh open her womb?

22. Ruth

My child, eat honey, for it is good, and the drippings
of the honeycomb are sweet to your taste.
Know that wisdom is such to your soul;
if you find it, you will find a future,
and your hope will not be cut off.

Proverbs 24: 13–14

I awakened ill and could not get myself upright without the nausea choking my throat, causing me to gag. Any of my stomach contents, mostly sharp-tasting, I threw up into the chamber pot. Naomi held my head, concerned, but with a knowing smile trying to perk the corners of her thin lips. I remembered how Orpah had been ill. "Am I with child? Or did I get some illness because I am tired from our wedding activities we had a few weeks ago?"

Even before Boaz and I had our wedding celebration, Naomi walked the distance into Bethlehem as far as the local Synagogue and prayed for an heir for Elimelech's family. She was praying for Yahweh to make some miracle happen since I had been barren when I was married to her son, Mahlon.

"Have you had a moon cycle since your wedding?" Naomi asked, looking at me with a hopeful expression on her wrinkled face.

"No," I said. My stomach pinched and I heaved, but brought up nothing. "It has not been so long, has it? My last moon cycle was about a week before our wedding."

"We wait and see," Naomi wiped my face with one damp cloth and stroked my forehead with another. She cared for me as if I were her daughter, saying kindly things to me. "You are a dear girl, and you will be a fine mother."

"If I am to have a child, it will be in the same year as Ammon and Orpah's." My thoughts brightened at the thought. I only hoped we would both have children who would be born well and stay well. I could not help but think of little Hester. When and if I had a child, I would protect it with all my being. Naomi smiled at my observation and I realized how much she had wanted both of us to bear children for her sons. It was in the past.

In a few days my stomach ills subsided, and I grew ravenously hungry. I noticed an ever so slight round-ness to my middle, and my breasts became tender. I met Boaz in the evening when he returned home. His fields did not need much attention as winter would soon come. While his properties now included all Elimelech had owned as well as his, little or no field work would happen until early spring plantings. We embraced warmly and he said, "I have missed you, Ruth. Are you now feeling well again? It is not yet finished, but I am having a mikvah made for your cleansing whenever you may need it."

I was not entirely sure how I would tell him what Naomi and I had decided was the cause of my ill health all these days. He was thinking my illness had been a painful moon cycle, or he might not have been prompt-ed to build a mikvah. I smiled, as I would use it even-tually. "Thank you, it is so kind of you to think of my needs."

He did not suggest we get our evening bath to-gether and we sat on a stone bench in the fresh air of a shade tree. The air had grown cooler lately, as fall was ended and winter would begin. I wanted to tell Boaz of our expecting a child privately before anyone else. Of course, Naomi already knew.

"I am asking Cook to bring our evening meal to us here under this tree, so we may have some time alone after being apart." He had hardly finished speaking when Cook and Silas came with a cloth and low table to spread on the grass beneath the tree. Next, they came back with plates, heaps of food on a tray, bread in a basket, and large goblets of wine.

"It is perfect, as I am hungry," I said. I lifted my wine goblet and he raised his as well.

"Shalom, Ruth," His eyes glowed with love for me as he lifted the goblet.

"Shalom, Boaz, I have something very special to share with you," I said, as we both took a sip of wine. I set down my goblet, and looked tenderly at him.

"What is it?" Boaz reached for my hand. The flecks of gold in his brown eyes captivated me.

"We are expecting a child," I said. There was no other way than to deliver the news plainly.

He was without speech for a moment or two, then reached out to me beside him and gathered me into his arms, pulled me onto his lap, and nuzzled my neck affectionately. "Ruth, Ruth, Yahweh has opened your womb so soon. We must go to Synagogue and give an offering of thanks to our eternal God and creator of all things. I suppose Naomi knows what she had hoped for is about to occur. Who knows what part our child will have in the history and future of our people? I think we are from a long line since Abraham."

We remained in our warm embrace, basking in the awesomeness of our great news. I was not barren, and we would be blessed with a child. My only concern was for the vulnerability of such a small life, and my responsibility to protect the baby from all manner of ills. He kept me on his lap and broke bread for both of us to eat, then gave me my goblet and we both sipped our wine. We ate our meal as we were both hungry.

Cook and Sarai were excited to hear our news. Naomi looked on with a knowing smile when Boaz and I announced at our evening meal the next day, and the impending birth was soon shared with close neighbors and servants.

A mild winter made the comfort of my growing body much easier than if it had been bitter cold or hot summer. The child would be born in early summer. Boaz became very busy in the fields as the planting began. Next, we prayed for rain to make our crops of barley grow. All the while my body took on the heaviness of the impending birth. It was all a new experience for me.

Boaz and I, with Naomi went to Synagogue and presented offerings of thanks to Yahweh and a sacrifice of two turtledoves. Naomi bowed her head and knelt a long while despite the age of her knees. She was murmuring Psalms and prayers quietly.

Another day, Naomi and I went to Shnayder in town

to buy soft cotton to make the swaddling clothes which would be needed for a newborn. Our hands would be busy anticipating the birth of the baby. The other matter was a birthing stool where I would have the baby. I remembered the one used when Orpah had birthed her child. Naomi said she would see to the making of one for me to use, and she spoke with a woman who often came to assist when a woman birthed. Naomi was excited anticipating a child being born to the family redeemer and me. It was turning out as she had hoped when she had sent me to the threshing floor long ago.

Boaz spent more time with me during these winter months. We savored the time. One day I felt a ripple in my belly. It was ever so slight, but I hurried to find Naomi, and then Boaz. It was real; my baby truly existed and waited to be born. Not then, but when the ripple became a little kick, I let Boaz put his hand on me to feel life with his hand as I did in my body. I did not know if it was appropriate as I had no knowledge of Jewish practices. We were in our bedroom. When he put his hand on my belly to experience the baby's moving, he had a look of joy in his eyes. "Ruth, how wonderful. Yahweh is great and has blessed us."

Naomi said the child would very likely be born in the month of Tammuz or Ab. At that time, Boaz would be working fields day in and day out as harvest drew near when barley and spelt fields would require cutting, reaping, gathering and storing. Some other fields would produce hay for cattle. I would not be gleaning or doing any work in his fields as my time would be spent birthing the child, then nursing and caring for it.

Silas was growing and developing into a fine young man, and did not look like the frail, ragged boy Boaz had first befriended. While he worked in the kitchen, he begged to work in the stalls with donkeys, horses and oxen. The animals loved him as much as he loved them. He shoveled out their dung, and put fresh straw in their beds and troughs. He liked going to the well to draw water for all the household uses.

We watched as he came into the kitchen with a tall ewer of water. I said to Boaz, "Silas has made himself very useful, and I know you feed, house and clothe him, but the time he ran away he wanted to earn money for himself. Do you every pay him in money?"

Boaz rubbed his beard thoughtfully, and said, "No, I have not paid him anything and neither has Cook. I suppose it never occurred to us since he is well provided for with no need for anything else. Do you think I need to pay him?"

I stood quietly beside frowning Boaz, wondered if what I had said offended him. "It was only an observation; I wondered if he would be happier if he were given even a small amount of coins in his pocket? It is your business."

Boaz walked away without saying anything.

23. Naomi

*When they came together, the Lord made her
conceive and she bore him a son.*

Ruth 4: 13b

My life was full. Boaz was our family redeemer, and now he and Ruth would soon have a child. I prayed fervently to Yahweh for a healthy boy. My thoughts often went to names to give such an heir. We could name him the same of any who were deceased, only not the same as any men who still had breath. It was against custom to do so as it became too confusing if two men were alive with the same name in a family. He would never be called Boaz. Boaz would give him a name at the brit. It could be he who performed the circumcision, or perhaps Rabbi Matteaus, or some other worthy elder among us.

Ruth was a loving daughter, and I thanked Yahweh she had come here with me even leaving her own people, and proclaiming she would worship my God. Her father was a believer in Yahweh, but her mother only worshipped Chemosh. I shuddered at the thought of how it may have been had Mahlon lived and they had children who would be influenced by such a foreign god by a grandparent. Yahweh knew everything, and how it was supposed to be.

"Naomi, I wish the time would come for me to have this child as I am so encumbered with my largeness and my swollen feet do not look like mine. I wonder if it is a boy or girl, and I pray my baby will be healthy. It feels energetic to me, as sometimes it seems as if the little one is running a race inside my body. Will it come out of me kicking and squealing?" Ruth was sitting in the sunlight coming in the window. It was already the month of Tammuz. She looked beautiful and radiant, hair and face aglow.

"The baby will certainly cry out, as it needs to breathe air. It will no longer be supplied with all it needs from your body, but must live on his own strength. You will nourish him at your breast, and do everything you can for him to raise him well. He should come out of you still and slippery, but soon will cry and perhaps do some kicking to strengthen his legs." I pictured the child, and thought of it as "he."

"Mother, I am so happy you are here with me. I do not know what I would do without your years of experience and wisdom, and of course, your love." She smiled and continued, "He will nurse from my breast after he is born. I sense their fullness now. How much will my breasts fill up, and how often will he demand to nurse?"

"My dear, Ruth, your breasts will provide as the baby needs the milk, and there will always be enough. Some children feed frequently, seldom leaving their mother's breast; others leave some time in between while they sleep and their mother rests. It will be a little different for each child, as it was for me. Mahlon never seemed to get enough milk, and my mother found a wet nurse to nourish him when I had no more energy. I was young, and my mother was very protective. When Chilion was born, he was different than his brother. I had only weaned three-year-old Mahlon, a few days and became with child. Blessedly, Chilion was content to nurse and sleep in between each feeding. It was always different between those two. Ah, memories." I suddenly felt tears begin to fill my eyes. "I must go see to Sarai in the kitchen. She limped more than usual when I saw her first thing today." I left Ruth sitting and smiling, despite her uncomfortable swellings.

As the day wore on to evening, and Boaz came home from his working in his fields, he went to be with Ruth who still sat comfortably as she could in the common room. He reached down to embrace her, and I looked away to give them their private moments. I went back to the kitchen, as I knew our meal would be ready soon. It had already grown late, but we had waited for Boaz.

The meal was being placed on the table and bowls of stew were ladled, bread in a basket, wine poured for us to enjoy. Suddenly, Boaz came into the room with a worried and surprised look on his face. "Naomi, Ruth needs you, or needs someone more capable than me. She cried out in pain and told me to get you."

I hurried in and saw Ruth clutching her belly and looking both startled and happy, and in anguish at the same time. "My daughter, I must get you to the birthing stool." Sarai came in and we two helped Ruth to another room where all was ready for the birth.

Boaz did not reappear as he knew birthing was not something he knew much about or could help with.

Sarai helped me remove all Ruth's clothing, and get her near, but not yet on the birthing stool. Usually first children were not born quickly, and we did not want her to squat for so long. "Are the pangs still far apart?" I asked.

Ruth nodded, lying on the mat, on her side. Sarai filled another basin with water and dipped a cloth to wipe Ruth's damp brow. "Shall we send word to Aida, so she can come help with the birth? We will likely need it with this being her first baby."

"Yes, please," I said. Sarai went out to speak to a servant runner to bring Aida out from the town.

Ruth closed her eyes, and her lips moved as if she were speaking, but she was not even whispering what she said. I saw her lips move again, and I heard her saying, "Yahweh, praise to you." I joined in with her prayer in my own spirit.

Aida, with a bag of items slung on her back, bustled into the room. She was ageless, not as old as me, but older than Ruth by some years. Her graying hair was tied up tight on her head and out of the way, but not braided. She knelt on the floor beside Ruth and spoke softly with her, asking about her pangs. Time seemed to stand still while we waited. Ruth began to pant and cry out. "Oh, oh, I have wet myself! I do not know what to do!"

"Come, help me get her onto the birthing stool. It is time!" Aida said. We helped her to the stool. All was ready with a wool lined basin to catch fluids from the birth. The baby would be in Aida's capable hands when it was born. I had a swaddling cloth lain out. Sarai brought a basin of salted water with which to bathe

the newborn, and to remove fluids, and blood.

Ruth cried out and gave one last push with Aida's encouragement. I saw the baby slip into her hands and wished I had been the one to catch him. It most definitely was a slippery, shiny baby boy! Aida gave him a slight slap upon his back and he wailed out loud and breathed.

"I want to hold him!" Ruth said, even in a weak voice.

"We will wash him first," Aida said. She handed him to me and Sarai poured the salted water over him to cleanse him. We used cloths to finish the cleaning. Ruth also washed herself.

Then he was wrapped tightly and I placed him on Ruth's breast. He had put a tiny thumb in his mouth. A clean soft mattress was already prepared for her and the newborn. My heart was soaring with joy at the sight of them. Yahweh had answered my prayers.

I helped Ruth into a clean robe. Aida and Sarai cleaned the birthing area. Aida bundled the afterbirth which was in the basin and readied it for its appropriate burial. I knew where I would select as its resting place, but I did not know if Ruth wanted a say in where it was ritually buried.

At last I stepped out of the room and washed myself, changed into clean clothing, then went to the kitchen. Sarai had already let Cook know all was well. "Where is Boaz? I want to tell him."

I walked into the common room. Ruth had managed to walk from the birthing room into the common room and she and Boaz were both holding the baby in their arms between their bodies. I decided I did not need to be the one to give Boaz the news. He had his son, and he had his wife. It was a beautiful sight. Yahweh was indeed good. Now I prayed all would be well with this boy child as he grew into manhood.

24. Ruth

*The women of the neighborhood gave
him a name saying, "a son has been born for Naomi."*

Ruth 4: 17

I gazed with awe at the baby in my arms. I was no longer barren, but a mother. He was given to us by Yahweh, to Boaz and to me and to generations on into the future. He was our son, and Naomi's answer to her many prayers. In the days following, neighbors came to call on Naomi, and were excited by her news as they remembered how bitter and sad she was when she had first returned to Bethlehem after losing her husband and both sons. They wanted to see the child and Naomi took him in her arms, cuddling him to her breast. My friend Miriam surprised me by coming to see me and the baby as well, stayed only a short while and gave me a small coverlet to wrap him in.

The women said, "Blessed be the Lord, who has not left you this day without next of kin, and may his name be renowned in Israel! He shall be to you a restorer of life and a nourisher of your old age; for your daughter-in-law who loves you, who is more to you than seven sons has borne him." Ruth 4: 14-15

It was soon time for our boy child to be circumcised. I asked Boaz, "Who will do the circumcision?"

"It will not be me." Boaz chuckled. "I would not want to cut anything I shouldn't. Since I have no knowledge of how to do it, I cannot trust myself. Rabbi Matteaus has agreed to do it. It will be eight days tomorrow since he was born. We will do the brit milah here. Naomi is excited, and has been asking me to name him. She suggested calling him Obed. What do you think?"

"I like Obed. It shall be his name if you agree." I said.

"I like the name as well. We will call him Obed."

He was asleep on my breast, but at the sound of his father's voice, he opened his seemingly gold-flecked brown eyes, and I thought he smiled. "Obed, you like your name, I see."

A sumptuous feast was prepared by Cook, Silas and Sarai. They were as excited as Boaz and me about Obed's brit milah being performed in our home. No one was more joyful than Naomi. Naomi dressed Obed in a new tiny white cotton robe and swaddle cloth she'd had Rebekah make for the day of his brit milah, the rite of circumcision. I had never experienced anything like it in my life, having been raised in Moab. Rabbi Matteaus came to do the honors for Obed.

Only the Rabbi Matteaus and Boaz went into the room in which we had lain Obed on a clean cloth. He had been nursed, wore clean clothes, and was quiet. I heard him only cry out for a moment, and worried he had felt pain. Boaz came into the common room, had Obed in his arms and was chuckling and jabbering to him about how good he had been.

"Why did he cry out? Was he hurt?" I asked.

"No, he is a brave boy, and what you heard was him objecting to the Rabbi taking him into his arms for a blessing once he had removed the foreskin. Matteaus is so quick and skillful with a very well sharpened knife. He has done thousands of circumcisions and would not hurt any child."

I took Obed and cuddled him to give him reassurance I would never let anything happen to hurt him as long as I could prevent it. Naomi held out her arms and I let her take him and hold him close as she loved to do. All was well and would be well.

We had a delicious meal. The Rabbi Matteaus complimented our family and repeated to Naomi what so many others said about the blessing of the family kinsman and her daughter-in-law. "The child may be destined for greatness, at least be the seed of future generations." He turned to Boaz and said, "Your father Salmon was from Nahshon, and they, you and Obed are from a long line of descendants beginning with Abraham. Had I the list in front of me, I could recite them all, but it would weary all ears at the table." He chuckled good-naturedly.

Silas came into the room with more food on a tray. Rabbi Matteaus looked at him and said, "Were you the beggar in town a while back? I am happy to see you have found good employment. If you ever get tired of Boaz and need another job, let me know."

"Thank you, I am very happy here, with food, a bed and clothing to wear," Silas said.

"And lately, I have been giving him some coins to save as he has been cleaning the cattle stalls, and taking care of horses and donkeys as well as helping Cook and Sarai." Boaz said.

We all talked some more about nothing and everything, and Rabbi Matteaus left. Cook, Silas and Sarai cleaned up after our meal. Naomi sat in a chair with Obed on her lap and hummed to him. They appeared to be content, but soon he would demand to nurse again. He was a hungry little one. I loved every minute taking care of him, but knew I had to share him with Naomi as she loved him.

Boaz and I went to the bench beneath the shade tree where we liked to sit and talk. "I am so pleased you could take the day off from your fields to do this for our son," I said.

"Nothing could have kept me from being here for such an important rite. He is our responsibility, our beloved son, and forever a son of Israel now; never any other."

"My father worshipped Yahweh, and told Ammon and me about his god, but we never went to a Synagogue. I do not know if there was one anywhere near in Moab. Although I do not know, I am fairly sure Ammon was not circumcised. My mother worshipped Chemosh as it was her family's practice. I was not sure who I should worship until I was married to Mahlon. Naomi's faith touched me, and I believed in her god, Yahweh. I thought Yahweh should have dealt more kindly to her, as he took away her husband and then both sons and even her baby granddaughter in death." I was quiet then, perhaps I had said too much. Boaz had a look of serene contemplation on his face.

"Thank you for sharing deeply with me. You have told me some of this before, but I did not realize until now how much Naomi influenced you in your faith in Yahweh. I have been thinking about what Rabbi Matteaus said to us today about our family history. I had not thought of it before. It is a big responsibility to raise a son, one who will someday be a father himself."

"I have to keep him safe, and I cannot bring him out very soon, for fear he could come in contact with anything which could make him ill and die. It was so very hard to watch little Hester become sick and die."

"We will keep him at home and safe, so do not fear." Boaz patted my hand and then held it in his big chafed hand, already worn from handling sheaves in the field.

Many days passed, and each were much the same for me as I was constantly caring for Obed. Naomi took over when I would let her, as she was besotted with him, and enjoyed each moment when he was in her arms. It was not long before he wanted freedom from laps and coddling. "Na," Obed would plead, pushing her away after she started to hold him tightly in her arms. She would relent and place him on a mat on the floor, where he would wriggle and squirm like a little worm until he had the mat wrinkled and bunched up. He would roll over and giggle and be off of it onto the floor. In a few short days, he was on all fours on the floor, and trying to crawl, and soon he mastered it. We were all thrilled. One day, too soon, I thought, he grabbed at Naomi's robe and pulled himself up to stand by her as she sat. She reached to pick him up and he cried out. It was not long after that he learned the word, "No."

His first word was, Pama, and shortly after was, Maha. Boaz was thrilled to hear him, so proud of our son. He took his first steps right after his first birthday. We both thought we could never thank Yahweh enough, and were so busy with our private lives and time with Obed, we did not see Naomi decline in health.

Naomi and I had not shared a bedroom since I had married Boaz. She kept to herself some days, and I thought it was due to the tiredness of old age. We always ate our evening repast together as a family. One evening she did not join us, and Sarai sent another servant to see if she needed any help. She came down, and apologized for being late, as she had taken a late afternoon nap. The bowl of stew in front of her and her piece of bread remained barely touched, and she was very quiet. Obed was learning to spoon foods into his mouth, and babbled as he spilled half a spoon of stew onto his clothes. He reached into the bowl with his hand to bring more food to his mouth. I sighed, knowing I would be putting clean clothes on him after our meal.

Next morning, I awakened after Boaz, and Obed was already standing on his soft woolen bed next to ours. "Ma, go Nani."

I changed him, nursed him, and we left the room. He wanted to see Naomi, so I went to her room which was near ours to see if she were still abed. I opened the door and saw her lying there peacefully. "She's sleeping," I said.

"Nani, Nani," Obed cried loudly. I could not shush him, so carried him to the bed where she was. I was going to reach out and touch her, but I heard no breath coming in and out, nor saw her chest move with breathing. He stopped his insistence and looked at me. I cuddled him, and began to cry quietly. He patted my cheek. "Ma," he said. I hurried downstairs to the kitchen.

"Sarai, will you see to Naomi for me." She nodded.

I wondered if what I thought was true. Had Naomi died?

25. Boaz

Train children in the right way,
and when old they will not stray.

Proverbs 22: 6

"Naomi is dead," I said. There was no other way to announce what Rabbi Matteaus had told me when he was summoned by our servant. Spices were brought from Bethlehem to anoint her remains. No one, except those involved in the preparation of her body for burial, would touch her body as they would become ritually unclean. The trusted servant who had gone to find out by trying to rouse her was a woman of faith and would go cleanse herself in a proper mikvah, and then spend what time was needed before she could be among people again. We would bury Naomi in her father's tomb on the outskirts of Bethlehem.

Ruth was mourning. We both had torn our sleeves and lamented. "I loved her so very much, more than my own mother," she said. Obed did not understand much about what was going on, but I told him his nana was no more, and had gone to be with her father, mother, and husband. I was not sure where our spirits went when our bodies no longer had breath, but I clung to the thought of an afterlife. He looked at me, and in his baby way of speaking said, "I go?"

"No, my son, you will not see her here again."

"Oh," Obed said. When he looked at me and I did not say anything else, he continued to stack some small blocks of wood Silas had fashioned for him to play with. When he had time, Silas would sit on the floor and amuse Obed, toying with whatever he was playing with. Ruth and I were grateful to have Silas play with him especially when we were busy.

Neighbors came and sat shiva with us for the seven days of mourning. We all went to Bethlehem to the cave which was used for Naomi's family. Since Elimilech and their sons were buried in Moab, it was the right thing to do. For me, the days went slowly, but I would not have shirked my duty in sitting with those who came to respectfully sit with us and mourn.

I was grateful for my family and often gazed upon the quiet beauty of Ruth sitting and nursing a squirming Obed. I loved them both, and was grateful to Yahweh for sending first her and then my son to me. "My son," I said the words aloud to myself as I loved the sound, and all it meant. Nothing could cloud my contentment and joy. Ruth was a good mother. When Obed started to toddle, using his chubby little legs, I thought it was wonderful. He began to say words and was fascinated with the donkeys and horse in the stable. Either Silas or Ruth was always with him, protecting him. He wanted to pat the donkey's muzzle.

"Are you never going to give our son freedom to roam?" I said, but not seriously.

"Never," Ruth said. "I have to protect him at all costs."

Soon he would be three years. I said to Ruth, "I would like to go to Jerusalem to Passover feast next year. All men are supposed to go to Jerusalem for the event, and in recent years, I have been remiss. This year I must go and I will bring Obed. He needs to see the temple and begin to learn more about his faith."

"I will make the trip with you, if you must go," Ruth said. "He may be weaned by then. It will be in the month of Nissan, I believe. Naomi talked about it when she was alive, and how her husband and sons had missed going when they lived in Moab."

"I want you to come with us," I said. I began to think of all the plans I would make for the trip, readying an oxen-yoked cart or a yoke of donkeys. Ruth could see to the packing of clothing and food. We would bring some servants to tend the animals, cook our food, and provide any general help we needed on our short trek. If I were going alone, it would take less than a day for me to get there, but then I would spend the Passover time there as prescribed by law. I would have to decide whether I wanted Cook to come, and which other servants to bring. I would rent an upper room or we would join the family of my friend, Nathan, in his home, and have our family Passover meal together there.

Adar began and with it, the planting of grazing crops which would be cut for hay when ripe and dry. Next, I was supervising barley seed planting, and hoping for rain. It was the same every year. Plant, watch the row upon row of green sprout, and then become golden grain beckoning in the fall breeze, and then we harvest the crops.

+++

We left in what I thought would be ample time to get to Jerusalem to the Temple for Passover. Our trek took most of a day, as I did not want to travel too fast with my wife and child to feed and care for. We stopped more than once to give our legs a chance to move, but mostly to give Obed time to get rid of some of his energy. He was not accustomed to being cooped up and had never traveled anywhere as Ruth had forbidden it until now. Even now, she watched him anxiously as if he would fall and hurt himself irreparably at any moment. If I said anything about it, she would remind me why she worried, how the family had watched her niece, Hester, die when she was a baby.

As it was dark by the time we got to Jerusalem, we decided to sleep in the cart beside the road where the shade of a tree would shelter us from sun in the early morning. I wanted to sleep under the stars on a mat on the ground, but Ruth would not hear of it. "No, I want Obed and myself to sleep inside the cart as we had discussed before we left," she said. She began laying out the soft woolen mat on which we were to sleep.

"Papa, I go," Obed tugged at my leg.

"I will take him outside while you get his bed ready," I said.

"You must watch him closely, as he gets off quickly sometimes these days," she said.

"I will," I said, as Obed reached his chubby little arms up to me, and gave me an open-mouthed smile I could not resist. I brought him out into my arms and set him on the ground.

Obed giggled and clapped his hands as I stood him beside me by our cart. He looked around, and I realized things must look different for him being so little. I was going to pick him up to point out Jerusalem skyline in the distance which was fast disappearing with the sunlight leaving. In a flash, he was running. I ran to catch up with him, but before I reached him, he tripped over a rock and fell. He wailed loudly, "Mama, Mama, oh, oh," Obed sniffled and cried. I picked him up and he looked at me but would not be comforted, and kept crying. Ruth climbed down, and rushed out as I knew she would.

"Obed, you hurt yourself. What happened little one?" She saw his tender knee had scraped on something and was beginning to bleed. She looked up at me and shook her head as if to say she should never have put him solely in my care.

Angry with myself, I stood helplessly, wondering what she would ask of me. What would I have to do to atone for my neglect, and would she ever trust the boy into my care? Would she allow me to carry him into the Temple for the Passover rituals meant only for the men and boys, or would she deny Obed and me the privilege?

26. Ruth

*Observe the month of Abib by keeping the Passover for the
Lord your God, for in the month of Abib the Lord your God
brought you out of the land of Egypt by night.
You shall offer the Passover sacrifice for the Lord your God,
from the flock or herd, at the place that the Lord will
choose as a dwelling for his name.*

Deuteronomy 16: 1-2

I cleaned Obed's leg, and saw my baby was not badly hurt, mostly scared and surprised to have his running stopped so abruptly by falling. He had been weaned, so my breast was not a place of comfort as it had been only a few short weeks ago. I put a nourishing goat milk in a small goblet and held it to his lips to drink. He took a few sips and pushed it away. I did hold him close to my breast then, and sang a song to him. His eyes fluttered, closed. I settled him onto a woolen mat in the cart, and gave him a soft cloth he liked to hold when he went to sleep.

Boaz had not come back inside, and I let him be. He was undoubtedly upset by what had happened. I was reconsidering my approval of him taking our little boy into the Temple, where I was not to be a partici-pant in the formal Passover selection of an unblemished lamb and the reading from the sacred scroll regarding the history and reason for the holy observance. We had plans for our own family Passover meal, as Boaz had arranged it with another family he knew which would share the meal as three people could not possibly con-sume an entire roasted lamb as was required. I did not know how I would approach my misgivings with Boaz, and demand he go without Obed. Obed was little more than a baby. There would be other years if the boy sur-vived as I prayed daily he would.

Boaz came inside at last. "I am so very sorry I let go Obed's hand, and he went off, tripped and hurt himself. Our son is willful and strong."

"And he is still a baby, weaned, but walking unsteadily. He has never fallen until today. He needs my protection. I cannot allow anything bad to happen to him. It was too hard to see my niece die. Perhaps we can introduce him to Passover with our family meal, rather than going with you to the Temple. You may go, of course."

Boaz sat across from me on our sleeping mat, as still and straight as I had ever seen him. He knit his brow, but he said nothing.

"There will be more years as he grows and learns more. You may take him there to required feasts and festivals when he is older. If I can protect him, he will grow into a man, one you can teach all you know about Yahweh and his people." I reached out to touch his arm, and he did not respond and pat my hand as he usually did. "Please do not be angry with me. I am his mother and I know what is best for him."

"I am his father, and I am as much responsible for his protection as you. I would like to lie down and sleep now if I may do so on this mat with you." The chill in his tone of voice was unmistakable. He lay down, curled up with his back to me, and closed his eyes.

I did not know what to do about my fears. Everything about traveling with Boaz, and being a mother of a toddler weighed on me. I could not sleep. I thought about the unleavened bread we were to have with bitter herbs when we ate the lamb. I had the herbs with me in the cart. The family of Nathan, with whom we were staying and having our Passover meal had charge of baking unleavened bread. Boaz, Obed, Nathan and Nathan's oldest son would choose the unblemished lamb to slaughter. When we ate the Passover meal we adults all had to be fully clothed, including our sandals. Many families removed their soiled sandals at the door before entering their homes. We would do so, and then carefully clean them and put them back on our feet. It was what Boaz had told me was customary. It was my first experience of a full Passover celebration, as Naomi and I had done the meal before, but always were invited to be with someone who wanted a couple more people to eat the roasted lamb.

The lamb's blood would be smeared symbolically on the front door posts as a remembrance of God's angels taking it as a sign not to slay the firstborn in the Jewish households. The firstborn of all the Egyptians who had captured and kept the people of Israel in slavery would be slain as a message to Pharoah of Yahweh's power and his insistence he let his people go free. Even though Naomi had probably explained it to me I had not completely understood its symbolism until Boaz told me.

I knew Boaz was devout and was determined to teach Obed how to observe all the laws of Israel. After what had happened earlier, and little Obed hurting himself by falling while his father had complete control over his son for only moments I thought I could not trust him again so soon.

Sleep did not come. I looked at Boaz, snoring beside me, unaware of my sleeplessness. In a way I was glad, yet I knew there was a chasm between us which had not been there before. It was not my fault, I reasoned, but his. He needed to apologize and tell me he would not take Obed to the Temple to select an unblemished lamb. I wanted him to say there were many more years for the boy to learn of Passover Feasts and other important festivals. Of course, I was a mere woman, not revered much as Jewish women were sometimes little more than a man's property. He did not have to abide by what I wanted him to do with our son.

I could not remember having such a fitful night since the time we were all worried about Mahlon when he did not return. In truth, our fears had been realized. Would my fears for Obed's safety be realized? Would he get loose in the pen of lambs and be butted or trampled? They were lambs, not full grown, but surely large enough to do damage to a baby boy. I became more and more agitated as I tossed and turned, trying to ease my thoughts. I prayed Yahweh would help me, but he was so far off and distant, with many other problems and people, I did not expect him to hear me. I had been conflicted between my mother's Chemosh and my father's Yahweh and had not established a faith until I had lived in Naomi's house with her sons. Their absolute trust in Yahweh had led me to believe he was the true God, and no other.

I still believed it. He had taken care of Naomi and me and now my life was good with Boaz. At least it had been until tonight when we had disagreed with each other. I worried how we would talk with one another going forward. Sleep would not come and relieve me of all my anxious thoughts. I was so tired I cried softly, simply saying, "Oh, Yahweh, let me sleep."

I snuggled up to his back, but Boaz did not stir. I lay there content next to my big capable husband, and hoped we could find our way back to each other again. I settled down with my eyes closed and my mind at peace, and went to sleep. The next thing I knew, Obed screamed out. I startled, and wondered what had happened while I was asleep.

27. Boaz

Restore us, O Lord God of hosts;
Let your face shine, that we may be saved.

Psalm 80: 19

I had sensed Ruth next to me some time during the night. I smiled, remembering again the first night she had lain at my feet on the threshing barn floor. Both of us jumped at the sound. Obed was crying out in terror, which I supposed was a bad dream. Ruth was up first, and reached him next to her in our cramped cart. "Obed, Obed," she cooed soothingly, as she cuddled him to her breast.

He was trying to tell her something. "Weg ow," and tried to touch his leg. It was still dark, as the sun had not yet risen. I reached for him so we could lay him on our mat and see if something more was wrong, or the leg he scraped earlier was hurting. I put him on our mat, but we could see nothing. I stood to get our oil lamp and I lit it. What I saw disturbed me. His little leg had become reddened around the scrape he had gotten when he fell. "Have we herbal ointment?" I asked Ruth.

"Yes, I rubbed his leg with what I have after he fell. I shall put more on it as I have nothing else to appease his pain." She added a cool wet cloth.

I felt more remorseful realizing I was to blame for the boy running, tripping, and hurting himself. Now I was very sure Ruth would not allow me to take Obed with me to the Temple Passover service for men. I wanted to impart to my son all our history, and how important it was to listen to our God. I said nothing, biding my time.

Tomorrow would be Passover eve, when we men would obtain and slay our unblemished lambs. The lamb's blood would then be put on the doorposts of our houses. I would smear some on our cart front for good measure. The next day, the first of our seven-day Passover celebration, Nathan and I would roast the lamb over an open flame as prescribed by the law and tradition. Women would see to baking unleavened bread and preparing bitter herbs to serve with the lamb for our Passover meal. In the Temple, we would read from the ancient scroll, the words of the Exodus from Egypt. It was exciting to celebrate with people who all believed Yahweh's word, and would give our thanks for bringing our people home so many years ago. We had dwelt here and grown as a nation, protected by him.

Day was dawning, Nissan 13. Tomorrow would begin our seven days of Passover. Each day was devoted to readings and prayers, as men assembled in the Temple. Some fasted as a personal discipline, but it was not required by law. Women tended children and visited with each other, having their time for prayers as well. Some elder women would sit in the back row of the Temple and listen to the readings. Young women seldom did, as most were occupied with their children and households.

I watched as Ruth rubbed olive oil and herbs on Obed's leg. His leg looked no better than it had when he had awakened us, as sunlight soon flooded our cart with its glow. "Will he be walking around today?" I asked.

"We will see," she said. He was drinking from a

cup of goat milk, and slobbering some of it on his chin, babbling happily.

"Obed, will you be up to going out with me today to see the lambs?" I asked.

He looked at his mother, then back at me. He sipped more milk before he answered. "Wambs, Papa, I go." He kicked his legs up and down to show me he thought he was well. I was pleased and surprised at the boy's answer, as I had not expected any from him directly. I was pleased to see his early intelligence.

Ruth shook her head in resignation. "Two against one," she said.

"It is not two against one. We ought all three be in agreement about our son's learning about his heritage. Obed, what do you say?"

"I go Papa." He giggled and wanted off Ruth's lap. She let go her tight hold on him and he threw himself at me. I caught him before another disaster happened. I took it for an example of how fast he would act without thinking. He did not yet have the experience to temper his movements with caution. He needed for me to watch and be ready for his every move. Perhaps he had not learned a lesson by tripping and falling, but I had learned. I began to think Ruth was right, the boy might be too young to comprehend and learn what I wanted to impart to him at the Temple. Would he now be disappointed and cry if I went to select our unblemished lamb without him? I had already asked him and he as much as said he wanted to go with me.

"How old are Nathan and Anna's children?" Ruth asked.

"I do not remember for sure, but I think his oldest son, James, may be twelve, at least. They have two younger sons, and a daughter, who is near Obed's age. We will meet them today if I get our cart on down the road soon. James will no doubt go to the Temple with his father Nathan. I do not know about the younger boys"

I watered the donkeys at a trough by a well and got them ready to pull us into the city. Once we were there, I drove us directly to Nathan and Anna's home as they were expecting us. Before I even unhitched our donkeys, James, their eldest, was out of the house and helping me. One of their servants took over and James helped me get Ruth and Obed from the cart.

"Is the little one your son? I think my father said he was named Obed."

"Yes, it is Obed."

"Hello, Obed," James said. He looked at me and asked, "May I take him inside to meet the family?" Obed reached out his arms to him.

"James, thank you, we will all go in if we may," I said. Nathan and Anna came out. She had a sweet little thumb-sucking girl in her arms.

We all kissed cheeks and they inquired about our trip so far. We went inside talking all the while. James had Obed hiked up on his hip and carried him into the house. "We are going to select a lamb tonight," James said to Obed.

"Wamb," Obed said. His younger brothers laughed.

"Hush, Obadiah and Manasah, you spoke no better when you were little, even worse," James said.

Anna had made a wonderful breakfast of eggs, porridge with dates, and bread. There was breakfast wine for the adults and grape juice for the children. We visited and enjoyed ourselves while the children sat on the floor and entertained themselves. The little girl, Martha, rolled a ball of yarn to Obed, and he rolled it back with some coaxing from James. I decided it was beneficial to have more than one child of different ages who taught and entertained each other.

Anna said, "Today you men and boys will all be going to the Temple to select our Passover lamb. Ruth, Martha and I will be here supervising the unleavened bread baking for tomorrow's meal."

"I brought bitter herbs, for us to mix and serve as well," Ruth said. "We need to bring them from the cart."

"Our servant will help you bring all your things in as well, as I have provided a place for you to sleep here with us for the night. We are a big family, but we always have room for more."

"Thank you so much for inviting us to stay. I am looking forward to a meaningful and special Passover celebration with you and your family. I will bring in our sleeping mats and our clothing," I said.

Ruth was smiling, and had not protested, so I decided she had resigned herself to put Obed in my care when we went to the Temple. James would be going, and Obed had already started following him, and listening to his every word. I was sure the boy would be a big help, as he was used to taking care of his younger brothers and sister.

A place in the common room was made ready for me and my family, and our clothing had been brought inside. The day wore on with some visiting and talk of our Passover celebration tomorrow. The children played together and included Obed. Both he and Martha were put to their sleeping mats for an afternoon nap. We continued to talk of our faith and how we would conduct our celebratory meal tomorrow. I felt more excited than I had for some time. My life was going well, I thought.

When it was time for Nathan, all the boys, together with Obed and me to leave for the Temple to choose our lambs, I sensed a shadow of doubt on Ruth's calm face.

"Shall you and I have a word?" I held her arm and guided her outside. "Do you object to Obed going with us?"

"No, I suppose I truly have no say in it," Ruth said. Her voice was icy, and without expression. She did not look at me.

"You said earlier you did not trust me to take care of him, and you did not want him to go with me."

"I do not trust you to watch his every move. If anything happens to him when he is with you, you will be entirely to blame." She turned away from me, and I did not know what to do; Obed wanted to go with me.

28. Ruth

A capable wife, who can find?
She is more precious than jewels.
The heart of her husband trusts in her,
And he will have no lack of gain.

Proverbs 31: 1-2

Boaz and I were not in agreement. He wanted our son to go to the Temple even though he was only a toddling boy, and I wanted him to wait a few years until the child did not require we watch his every move. Nathan and his sons were all set to go, and James already had Obed hiked on his hip to carry him. Obed was clearly excited, babbling about going. I hoped James would keep helping Boaz with him when they were at the lamb pens. The younger boys Obadiah and Manasah trailed along behind. Suddenly, the youngest of the two, Manasah, turned back. "I don't want to go," he pouted. "James doesn't care about me, only Obed!"

Nathan looked at James and said, "Put Obed down and let him be with his father."

James put Obed down, but Obed complained loudly, "No, I go wambs."

Surprised, I had never heard him put so many words together as I watched from the front of the house with Anna and Martha.

"We will see the lambs," Boaz said, and tried to take his hand. Obed wrenched away from him, and clung to James. James looked amused, but said and did nothing.

"Maybe I should make all of you boys stay here with the women," Nathan said. No one moved or said anything.

Boaz reached down and lifted Obed into his arms. "You are coming to see the lambs with me," he said. "I will take care of you."

"Why does he get to go?" Manasah asked, sulking.

"You have spoken rudely," Nathan said, "You will stay here with the women, but James and Obadiah are going with us."

Manasah, the youngest son, hung his head, and trudged toward his mother and little sister.

We watched them walk on toward the city where they would select lambs near the Temple. "Let us go inside. We have preparations to do for tomorrow," Anna said.

It seemed as if I were missing something because there had never been a time when Obed had been away from my side for more than a short while. Martha sat on the floor and played with pieces of cloth, sorting, and stacking them. Manasah sat across from her and toyed with the ball of yarn. He found an end of yarn and began to pull it apart. I wondered if he would then wind it back or he was doing mischief because he had been made to stay with the women. I did not watch, as Anna called to me.

"Ruth, come see the garment I have mended. It does not seem to be going together well. The boys are always ripping something as they climb and explore."

"I suppose I had better get used to it. Obed is walking, running, and soon will explore even more." I took a look at the worn fabric of the short tunic. It had probably been worn by James and now fit Manasah. "It has seen a lot of wear, and has been torn and mended many times, I see."

I picked up the thread and needle she was using to mend, and said, "Let me help." I thought about Ammon, my younger brother who often came home with tears in his clothes when he was a boy. I took small stitches, closing the rip as best I could. Anna had already gone to the kitchen by the time I had finished.

In the kitchen, a servant was grinding spelt with a stone in a stone bowl to make flour. All would be fresh for the unleavened bread we needed to bake. Anna asked, "Would you like to stir the dough for the unleavened bread? Please do not feel obligated as the servants can do it, yet the bread is to be sacred, and I often will do it myself."

"I would be honored to help," I said. I tried not to worry about Obed, and hoped James was helping Boaz take care of him. We whiled away our time doing household tasks and visiting. I discovered she was very near my age, only four years my senior, even though she had already borne four children.

"I thought I was barren before Boaz and I were married and God opened my womb to bear Obed. I was married to Naomi's son, Mahlon, and we did not have any children when he died."

"It must have been thrilling to discover you were not barren, as having no children brings shame. Not everyone thinks and believes the same way, of course, but generally barrenness is looked down on."

"It was truly a blessing to have Obed," I said. I did

not want to go into any details about my upbringing where it was not the same, and about my mother's belief in Chemosh. I wondered if Anna even knew I was from Moab. As we talked more, I realized she had heard I was from Moab, and how I had left there to come with my mother-in-law and consequently had married Boaz who was our kinsman redeemer.

We prepared our evening meal of lentil and herb stew. Soon our men would be returning to give details about the lambs. Preparation of roasting our lamb would begin for tomorrow's meal.

As they wiped their feet and came inside the house, I looked anxiously at Boaz who did not have Obed in his arms or by his side. I saw James behind Nathan, holding a sleeping Obed in his arms. I breathed a sigh of relief.

Sleepy-eyed, Obed awakened as James was removing his sandals. Obed cried, "Mamam, Mamam!" I hurried to him and took him from James, cuddled him close.

"My little Obed, you are fine now. You are with me. Did you see the lambs?"

Boaz had gone out to help Nathan start the fire to roast the lamb. They were going to slit its throat to slay it, and capture the blood in a vessel to smear on the doorposts.

I had heard the whole story many times, and yet I still had difficulty with killing an innocent little lamb for a sacrifice and then eating it in its entirety. My first experience with it was with Elimelech, Naomi and their sons when I had married Mahlon. I had sobbed alone quietly that evening as I did not want anyone to be upset by my lack of understanding. In time, I had resolved the issue as ritual, and tried not to think of the lamb.

Obed quieted, and saw Martha sitting on the floor, playing with cloth and wood toys. He got down, and was soon playing with her, as they babbled in their child conversation each seemed to understand. I smiled and went back to the kitchen with Anna.

I took a bowl from her shelf, and mixed together the bitter herbs we would have with the Passover meal. Everything was going well as our families got along amiably.

I smelled smoke, and knew it was from the controlled fire in the rock pit where the lamb would be roasted tomorrow. James came rushing inside, and said something in Anna's ear I could not hear. She looked alarmed and they rushed outside. I wondered what could have gone awry, but stayed inside to watch Obed, Martha and Obadiah.

"It's Boaz, he laid a hand on the hot stone of the fire pit and it is burnt and painful," Anna said. "He said not to alarm you, but I knew you would know in time."

"Let me get wine and oil to pour on his hand," I said, as my life pulse raced beyond its bounds. Anna had a vial of olive oil in her hand before I could think where to look, and then grabbed a vessel of wine which we were saving for the Passover meal. I ran outside without thinking about anything else.

29. Boaz

Hear my prayer, O Lord,
Let my cry come to you.

Psalm 102: 1

I wondered how I could have been so careless as to burn my hand, but I did not think the fire had been going so long as to heat the stones. As I lifted a log to place in the pit, I braced myself on the stone edge with my left hand to toss in the log. The searing pain caused me to scream out and drop the log to the ground, not inside as I had planned. I was ashamed and did not want Nathan to help me to a log to sit. He did in spite of my protests.

James rushed toward the house, but I called after him, "Do not tell Ruth."

Anna and Ruth both ran to me. Ruth had olive oil and Anna had a goblet of wine, "I can either pour this onto your hand or down your throat," she said.

I chuckled at her humor, but held out my hand for the women to administer the balm of oil and wine to it. The last of the wine in the goblet she handed to me to drink. Ruth kept shaking her head in disbelief. "Are you the lamb this year?" she asked.

"No, the lamb is tied there by the small shade tree. He will be slain and roasted over the open flame in a while." While Ruth had concern for me in her eyes, I could see she was not as enamored with me as she had been before. I could not think how I would win her back to me. Now she had borne a child, would she think it was enough, and we had done what Naomi had hoped for the line of Elimelech.

My hand pain eased. The burn was not blistering and only turned red where I had placed it on the hot stone of the pit. Ruth and Anna both went back into the house and I was glad they did as the small children were inside. I wanted Ruth to love me as she had before, and if something bad happened to Obed, she would have another reason to blame me. I struggled with these thoughts and wondered if my parents had ever had quarrels or differences of opinion. Theirs was an arranged marriage between their fathers as was customary. As I recalled my youth, I thought they may have loved each other as I never remembered any problems. I had sisters and one brother. My brother had died as had my mother when I was not fully grown, and I farmed the property which had been my father's and grandfather's.

It was time to slay the lamb. Nathan would do it and I would catch the blood in a bowl to be used to smear the doorposts. James had volunteered to do blood smearing, and Nathan had paused before he agreed amiably. I had not been the one to slay the lamb in the last Passover meals I had, because I was always part of another family with whom I could share the Passover. The entire lamb had to be consumed, and a neither single man, nor a newlywed and wife could consume all of one lamb in a meal. In truth, I had obediently gone to the Temple for Passover as it was required of men. Naomi and Ruth had stayed at home when I went, and when Naomi was gone, I had left Ruth at home with Obed and come alone to Jerusalem to the Temple that year.

All of Nathan's sons came out to watch the

ceremonious slaying of the lamb and then participate in smearing the blood on the doorposts. Nathan reminded them of the story of the meaning of blood on the doorposts of our descendants which prevented the angel of death from striking any young boys in the household. The blood smearing done, Nathan and I lifted the lamb's body onto the hot stones so the open flames could burn off the hair of his skin as it cooked whole for us to eat in our Passover meal.

I smelled the singed hair, the burning skin, and it was not a pleasant aroma until the meat began to cook and waft in the air. It was then I also smelled the oven's bounty of baking unleavened bread to accompany the lamb. We adults were to eat standing at the table, fully clothed, and our sandals on our feet as prescribed by the tradition of Passover.

Soon all was ready. The children were made to wash their hands and come in where they would participate in the Passover meal. James would stand with the adults, but the rest of the children were seated on mats on the floor and parents would bring plates of food to each of them to eat. But first, when we assembled we offered prayers of thanksgiving to Yahweh for our ancestors whom He had successfully freed from the Egyptian slavery. Ancient songs were chanted, and I could almost hear the sound of tambourines beating with our words.

I looked across at my Ruth as she kept glancing anxiously to where Obed sat on the floor with Martha, Obadiah and Manasah. She did not look my way at all. Anna began filling plates for the children as soon as prayers had ended. Nathan used a knife and sliced chunks of meat for them. I added herbs to the plates, and Ruth tore chunks of unleavened bread to put on their plates. Then we all ate. It was a solemn, satisfying meal, and we ate every part of the lamb, except the bones. I thought we would bury those as I had always seen done before. Nathan said the bones should not go to waste, and he threw them out in the field for the birds and other animals to consume.

The entire celebration at the Temple lasted a week from Nissan 14 to 21. Nathan, James and I went every day. I enjoyed the company of Nathan and his family, but all too soon, Ruth, Obed and I would be returning home. Ruth and Anna had become friends in these few days, and I was glad to see it.

We packed our belongings into the cart, and I watered the donkeys at the trough by the well. As I hitched them to the cart, James came around to help. "Thank you so much for your help and especially for the times you have taken Obed into your care. I am hopeful we can come visit with your family again when we come to Jerusalem for a festival."

"You and your family are always welcome here," Nathan said, as he walked up to see if I needed anything from him. I clasped shoulders with both Nathan and James.

Anna came out with Martha on her hip and Ruth had Obed in her arms. I would cherish forever seeing the joy on their faces. The youngest boys tagged along beside them. We all said our farewells with cheek kisses and promises to see each other again. I helped Ruth climb into the cart and lifted Obed to her. He was babbling and suddenly said, "I go Papa."

"Yes, you are definitely with me," I said. "I will lead our donkeys, and you take care of your mother inside the cart."

"Mapa, Mapa!" He waved his hand to his new friend Martha, and the family.

"Mapa is how he says Martha. He really enjoyed playing with her," Ruth said.

"We will come back to see them some time, Obed." Ruth said. She waved with Obed.

Nathan's family waved as we took off. Obadiah and Manasah trailed after our cart until the dust blocked their view. I could never remember having such a joyous visit as I did with them, and I had known Nathan before but not as well as I did now. He was a fine Yahweh-fearing man, and we were friends.

I had kept my view on the roads as we went on our way with me making sure the donkeys were keeping a good pace. It was cool and pleasant, and I wished in a way Ruth could leave the boy alone awhile and come join me up front. Anna had packed some food in a basket for us to eat along the way and we would find a place to stop about midday. My thoughts returned to the happy time I had with Nathan and his family. I truly hoped Ruth and I could have more children. If she continued to avoid me as she had the last several days, I did not think it would be possible. I prayed silently to Yahweh to give me patience and guidance, and lastly to bring us back into a loving relationship.

When the sun was high in the sky, I found an olive tree with an old gnarled trunk, which still had some gray-green leaves for shade. Obed was asleep. I helped Ruth down. "How is the ride back there? Would you like to come sit beside me when we start again if Obed is still asleep?"

She shook her head and put the cloth we had along on the dry grass, then set the basket of food on it. We tore chunks of bread and dipped them in the wine we had. I remembered how we had had our first meal together in the barley field as we sat on a stack of sheaves and I had shared my barley and wine with her. "Remember our first meal together?" I asked.

"Yes, I do." She looked up at me. "It was a long time ago." She looked away.

"Ruth, I already loved you then and I love you even more today than ever, but we are at odds because of a difference in how we do parental care for Obed."

She chewed thoughtfully on wine soaked bread, but did not say anything for a time, but soon said, "Boaz, I do not know how to resolve our differences regarding his care. I want to protect him at all costs, and you do not want to listen to my plea as his mother. I worry a lot about him." She frowned.

A light fluffy cloud drifted in front of the sunlight

briefly. We dug into the basket where we pulled out a round of cheese, and dried sweet dates, plums and figs. Perhaps I should have spoken, but I did not know what to say and I did want to travel on to get home before nightfall. We finished eating, and packed what we had not eaten back into the basket. We had no scraps to get rid of.

On the road again, Ruth went back inside to feed Obed as he had awakened. My thoughts about our relationship consumed me. It was all I could do to keep my mind on managing the donkeys pulling our cart. I was heartsick and did not know how I would make things right again.

30. Ruth

Do not hide your face from me in the day
of my distress. Incline your ear to me;
answer me speedily in the day when I call.

Psalm 102: 2

Starlights began to fill the sky as we rolled down the road, and I saw our home. I breathed a sigh of relief to see the house lamp-lighted and welcoming. Sarai and some of the servants had anticipated our arrival so we would not enter our home in darkness. Boaz first helped me down from the cart, then went inside and picked up Obed to carry him into the house. Servants would unload the rest of our things.

"I'm going to take the cart to its place near the stall and have Silas handle the donkeys. I will not be long, and will join you for a goblet of wine and some bread before we go to bed," Boaz said.

I went to refresh myself. My maidservant had a basin of water ready for me to wash. It felt so good to bathe the dust off my face and arms. I put on a clean robe and waited for Boaz. I wanted to talk with him, but I was not sure how to begin. I missed the closeness we had lost during the trip due to our differences in the way we wanted to handle Obed. I knew I was right as a mother to protect him; Boaz needed to understand.

He came inside the house and refreshed himself as well, then he sat next to me on the bed. "Shall we go out and see God's heavenly lights together?" He took my hand and we stopped at the kitchen to put bread in a basket and pour goblets of wine.

I gazed up at the skies and saw a flash of light streak across the heavens in an arc. "Oh, look!" I said. And Boaz saw it too.

"I believe it is a sign from Yahweh. He is pleased

with us for going to Jerusalem to celebrate Passover," Boaz spoke softly, and patted the stone bench for me to sit. "Unless you would rather sit on the grass. It might be more comfortable after our sitting all the way home. Thank you for going with me, and for letting Obed have his first Temple visit at Passover. I am sorry, and apologize I did not take your wishes into consideration."

In answer, I sat down on the grass, which had started drying due to the season, but it really was more comfortable than the stone bench. We put our basket of bread and goblets on the bench to use as a table. He settled with me and we each sipped our wine, savoring the sweetness. I was content not to talk, as Boaz had confessed he had not treated my wishes fairly. It felt so good to be home, and to sit with him and relax with bread and wine. "I am loving this moment," I said. Somehow Yahweh had answered my prayer for reconciliation. I reached out and touched his arm.

He reached out to me then, "Ruth, Ruth, I have been right next to you these days past, but I missed you." His arm enveloped me in his warm embrace, and he pulled me on top of him as he lay on the grass.

"I missed our closeness and love too," I whispered. "Do you think it would be possible for Yahweh to open my womb again? Seeing Anna and Nathan's joyful family has encouraged me to think we could be parents again, so Obed would have brothers and sisters."

"I love you. I would love to come together so that

we might have more children. I want to so very much, my Ruth, my love." Boaz voice was husky with emotion as our bodies entwined.

Glossary

Chemosh – The deity worshipped by many of the people in Moab.

Ephah – A dry measure estimated at three-eighths to two-thirds of a bushel.

Gazlen – A robber. (Yiddish definition)

Hora – A folk dance of Israel in which dancers form a circle, lock arms, and dance to the left or right with grapevine steps and hops.

Ketubah – The rite a couple promises prior to marriage similar to our modern engagement.

Mikveh – Mikva. A ritual cleansing bath, usually with seven steps into its stone interior.

Moab – A country across the Dead Sea from the country of Judah. Much of it is on a mesa.

Ossuary – A stone box used to store bones inside ancient tombs.

Passover – A holiday celebrating the time when the angel of death passed over all the Jewish families, but slew non-Jew's children in Egypt when Pharaoh refused to allow enslaved Jews to go back to their homeland.

Rabbi – Teacher.

Shiva – After the burial of a loved one, the family and close friends sat together for seven days mourning out of respect.

Spelt – An ancient field crop like wheat.

Yahweh – Sometimes written YHWH, the Jewish name for the Lord, their God, whose name they could not utter.

About The Author

E. Ruth Harder

The author grew up on a farm in Uvalde County Texas. She married Charles Harder (deceased, 2003) in 1957. She was a Technical Information Specialist at Lawrence Livermore National Laboratory until retirement. She achieved a Masters in Library Science from San Jose State University in San Jose, California. She says, "Critique groups and workshops of the California Writers Club Tri-Valley Branch help keep me motivated as I pursue my passion for writing." She is at home in Livermore, California.

Novels: *Hannah Weaver of Life*, 2015 Russian Hill Press

The Unbroken Thread, 2020 Russian Hill Press

Torn and Mended, 2023 Russian Hill Press.

Advances in Library Administration and Organization, Vol. 13,1995, published, *"Library Automation's Effect on the Interior Design of California Public Libraries."* Her poem *"Widow's Window,"* was published in the 2014 California Writers Club Tri-Valley Branch anthology, Encore. *"A Light in Every Corner"* is in the *2014 Word Movers, An Anthology of Creative Writings by Seniors.*

"Daily prayer and Bible studies and my Holy Cross Lutheran Church family keep me focused on what is most important in my life — the eternal blessings of our Lord and Savior, Jesus Christ."